THE SILENCE OF MOTHERHOOD

A DR. VICTORIA JONES SINGLE MOTHER BY CHOICE NOVEL

VICTORIA JONES, MD

 Friesenpress

Suite 300 - 990 Fort St
Victoria, BC, V8V 3K2
Canada

www.friesenpress.com

Copyright © 2018 by Victoria Jones, MD
First Edition — 2018

Edited by Roxann Stoski

All rights reserved.

No part of this publication may be reproduced in any form, or by any means, electronic or mechanical, including photocopying, recording, or any information browsing, storage, or retrieval system, without permission in writing from FriesenPress.

The events and characters portrayed in this book have been inspired by amalgamations of real events, but specific experiences and/or people are not meant to reflect actual persons either living or dead. Any similarities to specific individuals or their experiences is unintentional and coincidental.

ISBN
978-1-5255-2398-4 (Hardcover)
978-1-5255-2399-1 (Paperback)
978-1-5255-2400-4 (eBook)

1. FICTION, CONTEMPORARY WOMEN

Distributed to the trade by The Ingram Book Company

THE SILENCE OF
MOTHERHOOD

1
Hello Silence, My Old Friend

The loud silence that enveloped my house was foreign to the story of our lives. This was not a place where I ever expected I would be, although I had longed for it endlessly, especially in those early days. I had longed for it, and now I did not want it. In fact, I loathed it. How could my perfect life be disrupted by what I thought I had always wanted? I could hear it echoing in from the corners of my mind, in a voice that was all too familiar, that of my best friend Rosalee Crookman, 'Be careful what you wish for, Tori!'

A cat walked by, followed by another and another. I laughed out loud at the irony that was inherent in one of my oldest son's favorite memes. There stands an open door with a clowder of cats advancing into a welcoming house with a caption that reads 'We understand you are over forty and still not married!' Logan had reminded me on many occasions that this meme reminded him of me—his dear old mom! This was the stuff that comedy was made of and that I was filing away for future use. My first career choice had always been stand-up comedian. My current career, cancer surgeon, had only arisen from a passion ignited later in life. However, that was a different story for a different place and time.

I listened carefully and was amazed, as I always was, by how loud the sound of complete silence was. It seemed to consume the house in its entirety, and to ring loudly in my ears. I closed my eyes and let it take me over fully and completely. I acknowledged to myself that it was likely going to become a much more common part of my existence, and I was trying unsuccessfully to accept that. Silence had always been a friend I had turned to in time of need, however I never anticipated I was going to have to accept it as one of my few and longest lasting friends. I reflected on my favorite time to be alone with Silence, late at night and into the early hours of the morning. It comforted me, while at the same time it seemed to insist that I more deeply explore what he meant to me and what we could become together.

As I had done many times in the past, I relied on my good friend Siri to help provide me with what I needed most. I asked her 'What is the definition of Silence?' Siri rose at once to my inquiry. She brought Google along into the conversation, and he came up with an exhaustive string of websites, all vying for the definition that best suited my needs. I was impressed by Google's apparent depth of knowledge on the subject, although I knew he was just bringing the right people into the conversation— he had no real knowledge himself. However, I made sure that I praised him for his efforts.

My first discovery was that the use of the word silence in everyday conversation had been on the rise over the last ten years or so. How strange that in a world that was becoming smaller and smaller, and louder and louder, that silence was enjoying a swift resurgence. I wondered, out loud of course, if people weren't yearning for a return to a quieter time. I got up and began to pace as this often helped me think. I found it ironic that Google would select to epitomize the word silence by choosing to conduct his part of our conversation without sound.

My thoughts rushed back to my current situation; the situation I found myself in that had resulted in this need to explore the relationship between myself and Silence. It had been almost fourteen years of someone needing me constantly; someone needing me to the extent that I was unable to separate them from any sense or definition of who I really was, as a person and especially a woman. I had chosen to have my children on my own, unaware of the extent to which this would braid itself into my whole existence of who I was as an individual. It was a world that I was sure only I and other single parents could acknowledge—those who were truly alone in their quest to ensure a life where their children could rise to their passions and be all that they could be. I wondered if 'normal' families, as society liked to call them, those with 'two parent households' or those families where there had been divorce, felt the same way I did. It was one of those things that I tried to push to the side as it was not a question that one could ever answer. Had these other caregivers spent the last fourteen years of their lives knowing where their children were every moment of the day, day and night, knowing there was no other person who could account for them? I smiled to myself and thought not.

And now my children, once again, had left me ...

alone …

Both children had fallen to the lure of sleepovers, first one on Wednesday and then one on Friday afternoon. Muddled in amongst the flurry of thoughts that were swirling around in my head was the recognition that I was truly alone. I had spent years trying to convince myself in the silence of the late evening or early morning hours that I was enjoying 'alone time'. This, however, felt completely and utterly different. It was not even the same feeling that I had when I travelled for business and found myself separated in space and time from my children. I was alone in my own home! No one had told me when I signed up for the deal of single motherhood that I was going to have to deeply immerse myself in my children's lives, and then I was going to have to rip myself back and let them untangle and flee! I laughed out loud and thought about how stupid I had been to think that life would continue on forever as it had always done previously. It seemed so unfair that the times when we were just trying to survive, times we wished would end soon so that we could come up for air, would then abruptly exit our lives without warning.

My friend, Silence, was deafening. It was not, however, the first time I had been consumed by him. There had been times, both before and after I had my own children, when I recognized that I had experienced the same feeling. The strength of his intrusion into my existence was what made it so difficult to escape from this time. I could no longer ignore the other times and what they had meant. This was a society that assumed that motherhood was always joyful and ultimately fulfilling, to the exclusion of all other parts of one's being. It was not a society that was ready to listen to what motherhood really entails. It was not ready to head about the trials and tribulations of those who experience it every day, day in and day out. It was all right as long as no one spoke about the silence of motherhood that had existed for an eternity. I was about to blow the lid off that!

2
Thinking of Motherhood

My name is Dr. Victoria Jones. I am a fifty-three-year-old single mother of two phenomenal young men—fourteen-year-old Logan and ten-year-old Lucas. Of average height and weight, 5'6" and 150 pounds, one would be hard-pressed to pick me out in a crowd. At one time a natural blonde, my wavy auburn Ms. Clairol hair now fell to just below my shoulders. I loved the way the red-brown coloring of my hair accentuated the deep blue of my eyes that had been passed from my father to me and now to my two children. Additionally, all of us were blessed and plagued with a very fine, creamy complexion. It was the type of coloring that many dreamed of, as long as they spent little time in the sun. I was constantly harassing both my children to apply sunscreen as 'they were fair and they were the children of a cancer surgeon'.

Most people just call me Tori. Most people, that is, except my boss, Dr. Christias, who calls me Jonesy. He always says that people should have respect and call you by your last name. I guess Jonesy is his way of respecting me—not sure I can always see that. I live with two fabulous children, three sedate cats, a gorgeous leopard gecko, and a questionable notion that I have the ability to be wildly successful in both my professional and personal lives. As a cancer surgeon, I am constantly amazed by the strength of the human spirit that has been pushed to its limits, both physically and emotionally. It is my calling, aside from the stand-up comedian shtick which keeps rearing its demanding head from time to time. I excel at what I do, and it leaves me with a sense of purpose and accomplishment. As a single mother, I marvel at the end of each and every day that a social worker has not shown up at my front door to take my children and return them to their rightful owner.

The journey to motherhood, or not, is different for every person. I cannot even remember when mine began. I think it is like any great adventure—does it start with the initial spark of an idea, the full formed concept, the first objective and real step forward? Can a journey only be defined by the end goal once it has been achieved? I certainly did not know!

I remember thinking about motherhood, from time to time, as a surgical resident—never before. There was a full generation, perhaps two or three, as the history of female surgeons is not well documented, of women who had chosen surgery over motherhood. I had never understood this, and I did not think that I would ever entirely understand this. I was not even sure at times that it was a choice, as it didn't seem that to have both a career and anything else would be an option for female surgeons. At other times, it seemed as if it should be able to be distilled down to a simple decision between two all-consuming obligations. Most of the time it was just a fleeting thought, sometimes a feeling, but never all-consuming as I knew it had been for some women. The picture was either a male surgeon with a stay at home partner or a female surgeon dedicated exclusively to her career. Who was I kidding? Both were exclusively dedicated to their careers; men had the benefit of someone who was able to be consumed on the home front.

The first conversation I remember related exclusively to this concept was between me and a potential future employer. I figured I would lay it all on the table. I explained that if I did not have a partner by a certain age, I would be having my children on my own.

"How can you be a perfect surgeon when you have children, partner or not?" the Chair of Surgery inquired.

"I don't expect to be the perfect surgeon or the perfect mother; however, I know I can be good at both."

"I cannot see you working for me."

"I would never work for you anyways!"

And, as they say, that was that!

Certainly, there must have been a spark or even the creation of a plan prior to this conversation. I cannot honestly remember. Being a very private person and not having many female friends with children, most of the conversations were probably held between me and my good friend and constant companion, Silence. This is one of my most commanding strengths, and limiting weaknesses, the ability to have long, arduous, elegant conversations without ever saying a word. I obviously had conceived of a plan that potentially saw me as the sole parent of my fabulous offspring!

I remember attending a focus group of women who

were contemplating a life similar to mine. I was privileged to be included in this ensemble of brave, smart, pioneering women who were considering taking the path less travelled. This had always been how I envisioned myself as well! At least it was how I had envisioned myself since the heartbreaking loss of the only man whom I thought that I would ever love.

The meeting took place on a warm afternoon in New York City at the headquarters of Single Mothers by Choice. I leaned in to the conversation with high expectations for vibrant descriptions of women who would travel solo, literally and figuratively, into a myriad of new and exciting adventures. I began to feel that I most certainly was about to 'find my tribe'. The discussion started at 1:00 p.m. on a bright October afternoon, and I thought that within an hour I was going to see a sharp turn in my existence toward a bright and novel future.

1:00 p.m.—I looked around the room at women with a common goal, to realize motherhood at any cost, even if it meant embarking on the treacherous journey alone. These women would lead me in my journey, as they most certainly would have well thought out plans and would be well on their way to single motherhood!

1:05 p.m.—Introductions. I found it funny that these women were on average five years older than I was! How could these women still be thinking about this at forty? Well certainly they would have well-defined plans that I could learn from. After all, they had a lead in the race by about half a decade, on average. I sat back and prepared to be led in the right direction.

1:20 p.m.—of twelve 'sisters' who at the beginning of the

day were destined to be my tribe, I had excluded nearly half. The conversation had degenerated into one of 'how could I possibly do this on my own' and 'how can I achieve the fairy tale before my time runs out'? I remember feeling pity and anger at the same time. I wanted to scream, 'You are almost all over forty, this is not a discussion of a fairy tale; this is a discussion of the next concrete steps!'

2:00 p.m.—I sat back and wondered where my tribe truly was. I was not discouraged, as I knew the world was large enough to house these confused and desperate souls and those who had already made up their minds and were moving forward with the full force of their convictions. Certainly, if these women were only thinking of going down this road, there were others who had been brave enough to take the next step. I would dedicate my time and energy to finding these women. Little did I know, I would not have to look very far.

3

Can Motherhood be Unsilenced?

As I wandered aimlessly around my empty house, I wondered what my children were doing at their respective sleepovers. I had been alone in my own house so rarely in the last decade and a half that I failed to understand where my place was in this three-story mansion. I had walked through my house, by myself, hundreds of times before. This time, however, my children did not lie sleeping behind closed bedroom doors. As I passed by, I noted my reflection in the full-length mirror in my front foyer. My auburn hair, which matched the rims of my Kate Spade eyeglasses, was drawn in a loose ponytail, which elegantly exposed diamond stud earrings and a matching cubic zirconia necklace. I wore a black calf length sweater, open at the front over a V-neck red silk shirt with golden buttons and skinny cut blue jeans, which were tucked into high heeled black leather knee high boots. Given my profession, I wore no jewelry on either hand or either wrist.

I noticed how much my house reflected my life over the last twenty years, mostly through the artwork that lined the walls of every room. Every piece could be dated to a time, a place, and an idea about what the future might hold. I ran through them as I had so many times in the past and reflected on what had spoken to me when they had each made the decision that I would spend my life with them. They were varied, yet the same, with a certain individuality and strength that I appreciated in those with whom I chose to associate. I questioned the lack of commonality within this parade of pieces but marveled at how each was a reflection of a part of its owner.

My thoughts returned to where I was going from here. As someone who had always prided myself on detailing the story of my life years in advance, I was numb at the thought that I was now faced with the realization that this was only the first of many nights to be spent defining my own destiny. How would I unwrap myself from a life that had been focused on my dependents for so long? Again, I had longed for this time and now it came upon me unexpectedly and without fear or apology.

I thought of all the times that motherhood went unrecognized and unrewarded; all the times that motherhood was silenced. The strengths that I had seen in myself and others had lain silent while the world continued to unravel, obliviously, toward an uncertain future. I felt compelled to make others aware of the myriad ways in which silence shuts down motherhood. I wanted to explore how this beast raised its ugly head at every turn and impeded the path of progress. It seemed funny to me that the antidote was in the very process of recognizing what was happening and speaking about it. Speaking was the antidote to Silence! I did not know if this would prove successful, one never does, but a fabulous idea had started to percolate in my mind!

4

My Tribe!

The journey to find my tribe led from that small group of women in New York City concerned with their ability to do it on their own, and still reveling in the Prince Charming fantasy, to a group of women who were either trying to become mothers or who had successfully achieved motherhood on their own. It happened about six months later, tacked on to the latter end of a surgical conference I was attending in the same state, Colorado. I rented a car at the Denver airport, and following my conference at the Beaver Creek Resort in Vail, drove the two hours into the Rocky Mountains to the campground that was to be my home for the next week. It was a far cry from the elegance of the conference I had just attended, and I appreciated the chance to get back to nature.

I removed my beige Timberland hiking boots at the door. The cabin reminded me of a spider whose eight arms housed the sleeping quarters for the eager participants, myself included, while the body was a large, rotund central meeting place. There seemed to be women and children of all shapes and sizes extending into all reaches of the simple, but comfortable, accommodations. I knew I was in the right place, and the noise was deafening. By the end of the week I would be longing for the Silence of a room similar to the one I had just given up at my lavish resort. If this didn't scare me off my desired trajectory, I thought that it was unlikely that anything would!

There was to be no uncertainty and no fairy tales elicited from the mouths of these brave souls. On the contrary, these women were the perfect blend of optimism and instruction. Theirs was not a reality that was sugar coated; if anything, theirs was a path lined by bricks of hard work overlain with perseverance and exhaustion. They regaled the crowd, other single mothers with a spattering of a few who were still thinking of motherhood, with stories of insanity and survival. These stories I would have found sad if it were not for the fact that this was the stuff that stand-up comedy was made of. I reflected on my first career choice and filed these accounts away in the back of my mind.

A taller woman, who looked as though she had taken a magic bus directly from Woodstock into this new time and place, approached me from across the room. She had on a simple long purple dress, which seemed to flow directly from her greying locks toward the floor. Her Birkenstocks revealed fiery red nails, which matched her bandana. She wore few other accessories except for a deep purple sling embossed with gold stars and moons, and from which a small head emerged comfortably from the top. She introduced herself as Cassandra, Sandy for short. The small head belonged to her six-month-old son, Alex. They seemed to float as one across the central core toward a room that she announced was for thinkers and tryers, like me. She let me know that we would all be meeting as a group, in the central core, in about ten minutes. As I threw my purple Osprey knapsack and blue North Face ThermoBall jacket onto one of the bottom bunks, I looked back at the two of them and thought they made my dream of single motherhood look and feel somewhat easier.

I quickly changed into a long sleeved, blue V-neck shirt with matching jeans and a red hoodie. I brushed my long blonde hair and put in up into a loose ponytail which hung to just below my shoulders. I entered the central core where women were organizing themselves into a near-perfect circle. There were children here, there and everywhere. Again, I reflected on how loud motherhood seemed and wondered if this were indeed the place for me. I had always been someone who had a deep appreciation for my dear friend Silence, in all his forms. From the time I was a child, my parents had both commented that they had never met someone who had a deeper appreciation for the complete absence of sound. I drew energy from the stillness and calm associated with the tranquility of quietness.

A small hand grabbed the bottom of my red hoodie and pulled me forcibly towards what appeared to be my assigned spot in the circle. The hand was attached to a small girl who explained that she was five-year-old Hannah, and that it was her responsibility to 'put the mothers in their place'. Well, I had certainly been put in my place before, but never by such a small soul! She pointed to a small, Asian woman seated across from us in the circle and commented that this was her mother. She 'met' her mother at three months of age when her mother had travelled to Serbia to 'make herself complete'. I could tell that Hannah had heard the story many times before, that she loved it, and that she understood that it was a very important part of who she was. Hannah trotted off to put the others in their place, and I took my designated place in the circle.

I wondered how I was going to keep all of the couplings straight in my mind, let alone the names of each individual mother and child. Which mother belonged with which child and what was the origin of each of these small beings? How many were created by donor insemination? How many were adopted? How hard had their individual paths to this time and place been?

As if she were reading my mind, the woman to my right turned toward me and said, "My name is Teresa. I am a tryer, and I find this quite overwhelming! I don't know how I am going to keep everyone straight!"

"Thank goodness! I was thinking the exact same thing! You can call me Tori, short for Victoria."

She went on to explain that she was from the Four Corners Region. She was born and raised in Farmingham, New Mexico, a small community of about 30,000 people. She had been working for a small public relations firm that held contracts in several towns and cities in New Mexico, including Albuquerque. She was thirty-six and had been thinking about becoming a single mother by choice, SMC, for about two years. She had recently moved on to trying in the last several months.

Hannah's mother stood up and introduced herself as Cindy Lee. She welcomed all of us and cheerfully commented that she was ecstatic at the fabulous turnout. She introduced Hannah, who appeared to beam as her mother shone the spotlight on her. Hannah had been dropped off at an orphanage and Cindy Lee had known from the moment she saw her picture that this was the child she was going to spend the rest of her life with. In a move that made Vanna White pale in comparison, Cindy reintroduced her daughter. "I give you Hannah!" she exclaimed. The circle broke out into a raucous round of applause.

We continued around the circle over the next half hour. Mothers and children beamed with each subsequent introduction. In total, there were seventeen women and twenty children; one set of twins and two mothers with more than one child. The children ranged in age from six months to seven years of age, thirteen girls and seven boys. The reasons for choosing to be an SMC were as varied as the women in the group; however, the end destination appeared to sit well with all.

Cindy announced that there would be wine and cheese starting in about twenty minutes. Patricia, a slightly overweight woman with smiling eyes, long dark hair and a six-year-old son named Sean, cried out, "Why wait?" The room broke out in laughter and agreement.

Several hours later, we headed down to the dining hall. I walked along with Teresa and Lorraine, the only other Canadian in the pack. She had a four-year-old daughter, Gloria, and lived and worked as a lawyer in Vancouver. Lorraine explained that she had stumbled upon this bunch of 'common souls', as she referred to them, about five years ago—and she was never going to let go. Gloria held tightly onto her mother's right hand as we made our way down the well-worn path to our much-anticipated evening meal.

Dinner and the rest of the evening were spent with more wine and stories of the decisions people had made on their road to today, the trials and tribulations of single motherhood, and the great dreams each woman had for themselves and especially their children. They made it seem so possible, yet so impossible, all in the same breath. I began to experience the same feelings as when I had first been accepted into medical school and then into surgery. My first reaction was excitement and joy. This was quickly tempered and replaced by fear and uncertainty.

Over the next week, I learned everything I could from these phenomenal women. Although I had entered this journey with no reservations or doubts, I was unsure that I was going to leave this way. Sometimes I would experience waves of certainty that I would ride for a few hours, and then the noise would begin again. How could I make room for Silence, which had grown to be one of my nearest and closest friends, while letting in this new and satisfying disturbance? There were however, the quiet intimate moments that were interspersed between the uproar - a fleeting moment of mother and child just enjoying each other's company. This is what I had always imagined motherhood would be like—gentle and quiet. I knew that this was naïve; that there would be days and nights filled with noise. However, what I saw in those quiet moments was just enough to cement my path. I intuitively knew that I had found my tribe.

5
Silenced by the Knife

The first communication, a Bitmoji, came from my oldest son, Logan, at around 8:20 p.m. My difficult visit with Silence was broken by a small, nearly exact replica of my son, which beamed up at me from the screen of my iPhone. 'How's it goin?' he inquired. I set my phone down while I thought about the most appropriate response, given my circumstances. There were a myriad of ideas expanding to fill all the corners of my mind. How was I going to bring attention to the silence of motherhood? Again, I laughed out loud. Certainly, my son was not asking me to regale him on my desire to change the future course of motherhood; to tell him that I was tired of the silence that I had always joyously invited into my life. How would one even phrase this by text, emoji or Bitmoji? Should I send an email? I noticed that I was starting to enjoy this brief reprieve from my battle with Silence. This was my struggle, and it did not involve my oldest son. I picked up my phone and texted back 'I am great! How about you?'

I was not unfamiliar with big challenges or great struggles. In fact, I knew that it was one of my truest strengths—I yearned for the advances of a significant hurdle and seemed to wither when not faced with some type of looming oppression. I vividly remembered the day I had learned that not everyone is like me in this respect. I had been attending a symposium for future leaders in surgery when the facilitator asked who liked to be in charge when push comes to shove or when the rubber hits the road. I aggressively raised my right arm and gave the 'pick me, pick me' wave, expecting that I would have to get in line behind a whole herd of other individuals in the room. I felt confused and embarrassed when I realized that I was the only thing standing between the question and a room full of silence. Needless to say, I was chosen for the part after my outstanding audition. I asked others why they chose not to rise to the occasion. I was met by a flurry of unexpected responses basically detailing the same theme. Many did not like to be in charge when it really mattered; they did not like a significant challenge. It was one of those defining moments in life.

I poured myself a glass of my favorite white wine, an Australian Sauvignon Blanc, and sat down in front of my computer to begin at Chapter One. The idea that Silence would be broken through words, by telling stories, was starting to meld into a concrete plan. My goal was to break the silence, and my intention was to brainstorm as many ways as possible to make this a reality. I decided that one of the strategies would be to enjoy a second glass of my favorite white wine. I sat down on the sofa to relax and contemplate my next steps.

I awoke an hour later. I had sat down to enjoy an episode of Rookie Blue, define my swift path to action, and had promptly fallen asleep. The telltale drool was readily

Silenced by the Knife

apparent on my cheek as I attempted to recover my numb left arm from underneath me. No matter how many times I tried to tell myself that 'being up all night + wine ≠ falling asleep without provocation', I could not break this equation. The fact that I had been up all night on call for trauma the previous night did not interfere with the idea that I was going to change the world.

I reflected back on my previous evening on call. I was immediately struck by the fact that I had been front and center in watching a young woman, a young mother, become silenced before she even had the opportunity to get to know her own children. The first story in my anthology had unraveled right before my very eyes!

It was approximately 1:00 a.m. and I was just returning to my call room after a very long and difficult operation where we had been trying to relieve an intestinal obstruction for over two hours. We had just delivered the patient to the recovery room, and I was leaving to speak with the family. The all too familiar warning came over the hospital-wide paging system, 'Trauma team to the trauma room stat! Trauma team to the trauma room stat!' I motioned to the residents that they should proceed directly down to the trauma bay. I asked the recovery room nurse to let the family know that their loved one had done fine during their surgery and that I would speak with them as soon as I could. I followed closely behind my residents.

Upon entering the trauma bay, we were faced with a young, female patient who had already been intubated by the paramedics. It was apparent, by the flurry of activity surrounding her, that she was in a bad way. The paramedics relayed to us that she had been stabbed in the chest and abdomen multiple times by her husband, in front of their seven- and five-year-old children. They estimated that she had been stabbed approximately twenty minutes ago, and she had been alert and speaking to them when they arrived. They had intubated her just as she rolled in through the doors of the trauma bay and now she had very faint pulses.

"We have no pulse!" yelled one of the nurses near the head of the bed.

"Start CPR!" commanded the leader of the trauma team just off to my right at the foot of the bed.

"Get me the thoracotomy tray!" demanded the senior surgical resident, Bradley Simmons, as he donned his trauma attire, including sterile gloves. "Call cardiothoracic surgery and let the OR know!"

The set up was swift and well-rehearsed. The thoracotomy tray was opened and Bradley swiftly and precisely carved a twenty-five-centimeter incision from front to back, deftly opening the patient's left mid-chest. He placed the rib spreader and spread it from five to ten to fifteen centimeters in less than ten seconds. He placed a large intravenous line directly into the patient's heart as I donned my gloves and grabbed the suction to provide him with greater exposure.

"Run the blood as fast as you can!" Bradley commanded while compressing the heart directly between his two gloved hands while stabilizing the IV. "The heart is empty! I am going to cross clamp the aorta and see if we can't get a pulse!"

Bradley reported that the patient's heart had begun to beat spontaneously, and someone shouted from the head of the bed, "I've got a carotid pulse!"

"Let's continue with the blood and get her ready for the OR," I commanded, leaving Bradley to continue to stabilize the patient's heart and prepare himself for the transport.

I marveled, as usual, as the team worked as a well-oiled machine to get the patient ready for the operating room. Within ninety seconds, the team was ready for transport just as the cardiothoracic surgeon walked through the doors. We briefly explained the situation to her as we moved, in unison, towards the OR.

Just as we exited the doors of the emergency room, Bradley shouted, "The heart is not beating. It feels full, but it is not beating! I am starting internal compressions!"

We decided to move down the hall to the operating room. By this time, anaesthesia had joined us, and they were getting prepared to take over care of the patient's airway.

Blood started to pour out of the left chest just as we crossed the threshold into the operating room. Bradley stopped internal cardiac massage and reported that the heart was still not spontaneously moving. He restarted massage.

"How long has she been down?" the cardiothoracic surgeon, Dr. Lukas, asked.

"About an hour!" I replied.

"Continue massage," Dr. Lukas commanded, "I am going to scrub. Get her prepared for a clamshell."

A clamshell is essentially a procedure used to gain access to both chest cavities. The left chest incision would be extended across the front of the chest and all the way to the back of the right chest. The patient would be opened completely, lifting the entire front half of the upper body up and off the lower half, just like a clam. The patient was swiftly prepared and draped.

"Knife!" commanded Dr. Lukas. She completed the clamshell in less than sixty seconds and the patient was separated with two rib spreaders. Blood poured out of the right chest cavity and Dr. Lukas, Bradley and I placed multiple packs deeply within the right chest cavity to try and contain the bleeding. The anaesthetic team worked to provide enough blood flow for us to continue.

"We are losing her!" Dr. Swiftlee, the most senior member of the anaesthetic team, announced. "Continue internal massage!"

"The heart is empty! We need more fluid!" exclaimed Dr. Lukas.

"Carrie, we have been down for over an hour and the heart is empty. We have transfused over sixty units of blood and have activated the massive transfusion protocol." Looking directly at her, I announced to everyone in the room, "What is the end point here?"

"There is likely a supradiaphragmatic aortic injury. Give me more fluids, continue internal massage and give me fifteen minutes."

I wasn't sure that was the best decision; however, it was the correct one for Dr. Lukas, and I decided to go with it.

Thirteen minutes along, the main injuries had been identified and clamped to prevent further bleeding. There was no further blood loss, however the patient still remained unstable, and Bradley had now taken over performing internal cardiac massage once again.

"Stop internal massage!" anaesthesia commanded.

Silenced by the Knife

Bradley stopped and withdrew his hands. We all watched as the heart, filled with donated blood and other blood products, attempted to beat on its own. With each uncoordinated quiver, we urged the heart on. Our encouragement fell on deaf ears.

"Continue internal massage," I said to Bradley. "We are now almost an hour and a half into this with no discernable cardiac activity and with all bleeding controlled. There are no other injuries and anaesthesia has replaced all blood products through the transfusion protocol. The patient is not exceptionally cold. I suggest that this is futile."

The room was quiet. Bradley did not look up as he continued internal cardiac massage. I was wondering who would be the first to speak, the first to either support or refute my position.

"I agree," Dr. Lukas replied.

Bradley looked up, and while continuing internal massage replied, "I concur."

Dr. Swiftlee just nodded at me. He looked at Bradley and said, "Stop cardiac massage."

Bradley removed his hands and we all just stood there quietly looking at the heart. The nurses were the first to move, starting to gather clothing and other effects as evidence. They were more than familiar with the protocol, and that the police officers outside the operating room would be waiting to hear from us.

"I will go," I offered. "Bradley, can you try to get the medical examiner on the line, please?"

"Sure."

As I had left the operating theatre my mind had

wandered, as it was again now, to the two children who would never hold or speak to their mother again. This would be the first story in my novel. It was a very raw example of the fragility of the mother-child relationship and how it could be so quickly and easily silenced.

6
A Way Forward

The second communication arrived at 10:10 p.m. just as I had completed the first chapter of my proposed novel. It was my youngest son, Lucas, who was prompting, 'Can I stay over at Robert's house for the entire weekend? His mother says it is all right'. I knew there was likely a fifty-fifty chance this was anywhere near the truth. I texted Robert's mother to confirm, and surprisingly, she confirmed my youngest son's wishes! I snapchatted Lucas, 'Fine!' I was confident that I would maintain the Mother of the Year Award. I had won this award for the last ten consecutive years in a row, voted in as best mother by the two residing judges—my sons!

I returned to my computer and decided that I was going to dedicate a good solid hour to writing before turning in for the evening. Besides the short cat nap, I had been up for almost forty hours. I convinced myself that 'wine + lack of sleep = coming up with the best ideas to change the course of motherhood and the world'.

There were so many stories to be told, and they were not all mine to tell, although I could give other mothers a definitive voice. I wondered if I could even begin to scratch the surface with the ways in which I was thinking about this. I had never before had an idea that I was so passionate about, and I had decided that I was going to write an entire novel of stories, not just a short compendium.

The moment it surfaced into my reality, I knew it was right thing to do. I glanced down at the time on the screen—11:55 p.m. That had taken a good fifty-five minutes! Although I had made an important decision, I had only managed to write three words on the screen—WRITE A NOVEL. At a rate of three words per hour, I was definitely headed for quick success as a writer! I jotted down two more items and shut down my computer for the evening. I would need more than a little beauty sleep if I were going to pursue this for real.

7
A Single Mother by Choice

The journey to becoming a single mother to Logan, now fourteen, and Lucas four years later, was relatively easy once I recognized that fear of the unknown and the belief in fairy tales were not a part of who I was or ever would be. I had found my tribe and I would evolve, over time, to be one of them.

There was a myriad of sperm donors to choose from, every make and model one can imagine! I knew there were certain required traits. I had wanted my offspring to have my rich blonde hair colouring, my piercing blue eyes and my pale and creamy skin. Beyond that, I hoped for some degree of intelligence. The one thing I was looking for was a donor whose offspring would not be a klutz, would not be chosen last for the (insert name of sports team here)—who basically had some athletic ability. I found it amusing that there were some people who spent an eternity pondering over potential donors. I spent exactly twenty minutes. In my mind, it was one of those things where you never really knew what you were going to get. Spending more time and effort was not going to change that. Someone was not going to knock on my door one day and say, 'Victoria Jones, we are here to award you the trophy for choosing the best sperm donor vintage'. This was definitely not that!

I put in my order on a Monday and the goods were delivered directly to the local sperm bank on Friday of that very same week! What service! Six vials of my potential future offspring just waiting for an opportunity. The obstetrician, a good friend of mine, merely said, "Just call me when you need me and I will meet you at my office." There was to be nothing more than tracking with an ovulation predictor and making a call for insemination at the appropriate time. We would start simple and escalate as needed. There was little talk of 'maternal age' or possible problems associated with being 'an older mother'. I was almost thirty-eight at the time.

Fast forward about five weeks when I found myself staring at a positive home pregnancy test. That was easy, perhaps too easy. Fast forward another two weeks and I was sitting with my obstetrician discussing prenatal vitamins, prenatal testing and the timing of everything that was about to happen. This was perfect, everything in an orderly fashion. There would be blood work, an ultrasound at about eight weeks to examine the thickness of something called the nuchal ridge, and close surveillance due to my 'advanced maternal age'.

Fast forward to the eight-week ultrasound. There had been an ongoing and lively debate between myself and my obstetrician. These types of debates almost always happen when those on both the physician and the patient sides of the equation have been formally trained in the medical profession. I desperately wanted chorionic villus sampling, CVS, a new technique recently made available to patients. A small sample of the placenta would be taken for analysis. Genetic assessment, formerly performed at over sixteen weeks by amniocentesis, could now be performed at about ten weeks. She was concerned about the reports, although rare, of finger loss in the fetus as a result of the procedure. I retorted that it was a very small chance. Besides, there were many successful individuals, including physicians, who did not have all ten fingers! The debate was spirited, with both of us standing our ground. We settled on chorionic villus sampling if the eight-week ultrasound was abnormal, specifically if the nuchal ridge was thickened. Both of us were convinced that this would not be the case.

She counselled me as the ultrasound began. It would take about ten minutes and she had performed hundreds, even thousands, of this type of exam previously. She reassured me that the ultrasound would likely be normal. She seemed almost gleeful as we started. For me, it was just another step in the process of getting to where I wanted to be.

I followed the lines of her face, concentrating intently on her eyes and the corners of her mouth, as she passed the probe over my naked abdomen. Her pupils dilated and the corners of her mouth turned down. It reminded me of the phrase 'upside-down smiley face'. This was a phrase that I had used many times before when instructing residents on a certain surgical procedure. 'Make the incision as an upside-down smiley face', I would say, while thinking and sometimes even commenting out loud, 'I don't know why I call it an upside-down smiley face when we all know it is a frown'. Goddammit, I know a frown when I see one! I moved my eyes back up to meet hers. I knew instinctively that something was wrong, devastatingly wrong I surmised. She stammered, "It's, it's, it's.... not normal."

"I know," I said, as I comforted her by laying my hand on her shoulder. I sat up to hug her. "It's going to be all right," I commented. "We have a plan. Abnormal ultrasound and I get chorionic villus sampling."

I had won the battle, however I feared I was going to be losing this war.

8
The Silence of Motherhood

The chorionic villus sampling was scheduled for two weeks into the future. Although I was no stranger to misfortune, having suffered the loss of a significant relationship and a close family member during my surgical residency, the wait for confirmation of my known fate was almost unbearable. At every interaction, I thought about how many others around me were holding potentially devastating secrets, close to their hearts, that no one else knew about. I methodically carried out my normal activities—evaluating patients, performing surgeries, comforting patients and family members. I found myself wondering, many times per day, how ironic it was that I was the one closest to the brink. Who was there to save me? Who was there to comfort me?

Monday ... Tuesday ... Wednesday ... Thursday passed. By Friday of the first week following the CVS, I could sense that something else was not right. I was on call, attending to a sick patient who was being transported to the operating theatre for an emergent, and potentially lifesaving, abdominal operation. I excused myself, as I was not feeling well. I told the rest of the team that I would meet up with them in the operating room. At first, I thought it was just my period, and my mind focused on the operation I would be performing in a few short minutes. I was going through the normal actions of dealing with this ill-timed occurrence, when my mind was drawn abruptly back to the fact that I was pregnant. 'I am pregnant and the fetus is not normal, I am pregnant and the fetus is not normal'. These words kept running through my mind as if they were emanating from a scratched record, which was doomed to repeat itself over and over in my mind.

I did what I am sure thousands, if not hundreds of thousands, of women before me had done. I cleaned myself up, and I went on with the responsibilities of my professional life. I greeted the nurses, the other physicians and the patient. I held the patient's hand as he went off to sleep. I guided the resident through the operation, the removal of a segment of dead intestine, as I had done so many times previously. I saved this man and two more people over the course of the night, while at the same time I knew there was another potential life that I could not save. I was living both lives, my lives, in parallel that evening. I thought about how often women had been required to live this reality over the course of history. I wondered how many women I crossed paths with that same evening were either living, or had lived, this same experience, in silence like myself. I wondered how many had suffered. This definitely was not the Silence that I had grown close to in the past; the Silence I considered to be one of my best and closest friends.

By the following morning, the cramps were unbearable. Luckily, I had only three meetings that I had to sit through. I had taken a combination of Advil and Tylenol in an attempt to quell the physical and emotional pain of what lay in front of me. I sat slumped over in my chair, wearing the same scrubs from the previous evening. I was thankful that I had gone without sleep the night before, as all my thoughts and feelings were muted. The course of my outside and inside lives seemed to be melding back together once again, although the combination would continue to remain silent to the outside world.

The second meeting was probably the most difficult. I was mentoring a young female surgical resident on work-life balance, something I did often. I did not feel specifically qualified to do so at that moment. I could hear myself talking about 'finding your passion' and 'defining your own path'.

"What about children?" she inquired.

"What about children?"

"Do you ever plan to have any? I know that I think about it all the time and how I am going to balance things. I have always pictured children as a part of my life. If I can't have it all, I am not sure the surgery thing is for me."

I reflected on this comment. I knew that every surgical trainee reflected continuously on whether surgery was for them—were they up to the challenge, would they be able to do it, would they be able to have a life, etc.

"I think anything is possible," I heard myself say, almost from a distance. "I think that you have to be brave enough to think outside of the box and imagine how you might forge a path leading to what is important for you. If children are a part of that, then you will find a way to make it so."

I was at once fascinated and angered at myself for

uttering these words. How could I be so certain about this when there was a part of my path which was being redirected even as we spoke? As always, I toyed with how much of my truth to reveal in order to provide some clarity to people, especially other women. I decided against divulging anything today as I selfishly decided that this was my day, my fate, and nothing was going to stand in the way of that.

She seemed reassured by our conversation and had decided that she was going to persist. As she turned to leave, she paused, looked back and said, "Thank you for making me see that I should give Gen Surg another chance."

"You are welcome!" I wondered if she saw me flinch at the use of the abbreviation Gen Surg. As I always said to my trainees, 'Gen Surg makes it sound like a party or a night out on the town. General Surgery is a career, a profession, a calling'. Again, I decided against saying anything.

I made my way down the hall to my third meeting, acutely aware of my situation and the change in the direction of my life path that was being uncontrollably forced on me in that very moment. I thought it was rather ironic that my annual performance review, a review which would define my academic life for the next year, was being thrust on me at the same time that my personal life was in a state of acute turmoil.

Dr. Christias, the Department Chair of Surgery, greeted me at the door to his office. He asked how I was.

"Fine," I lied. "I had a busy night on call, and I am looking to wrap up a few things before heading home." I hoped that my sleep deprivation, heartbreak and anger would not be interpreted as a lack of interest in my academic performance review. Luckily, I had a past within the Department of Surgery and the university that suggested otherwise.

We spent the next half an hour reviewing my curriculum vitae, bio-sketch, academic portfolio and goals. I was always impressed with how organized and logical Dr. Christias was in terms of my path to academic promotion. In some respects, I found him aloof and disorganized, however this was one area where he shone. As the time progressed, I found myself reflecting on the meeting with my resident and wondered whether I had been as effective. I commented that one of my goals should be to be more aware of how and why I was mentoring residents and to really aim to set goals for my meetings with them.

"That's an interesting goal. Do you think it is easy or feasible to set goals in a mentoring relationship?"

We bantered back and forth about this for a while and decided that the discussion was for another day. I was to contemplate how I might see this unfolding.

"Thank you for meeting with me today, Jonesy. You seem somewhat distracted, but I am just going to chalk that up to lack of sleep. I think that you are well on your way to promotion to Associate Professor, and we should meet annually to discuss the process and ensure you are on track."

As I got up to leave, I thought about how many conversations women should have had about motherhood or impending motherhood had been derailed by someone assuming they were distracted, lacked sleep or otherwise. I thought it was probably too many to count. It definitely was not a discussion that I wanted to have today or anytime in the immediate future.

I took respite, as I always had, in the calm smooth air of late summer as I traced the paths through the forested area outside the back of the hospital. I thought about how many others in generations past had experienced the landscape in much the same way, with the beauty of nature remaining relatively unchanged throughout the passage of time. The smell of the air was soothing and seemed to envelop me in a way that confirmed that at some point far in the future everything was going to be okay.

I left work, after rounding on my patients, at 1:00 p.m. I called my obstetrician who took my call right away. I was not looking for an explanation of 'what is happening?', I was looking for 'how long is this going to last before this is over?'. She told me it was likely almost over now. I should get some rest and she would meet with me next week to speak further.

"When can I try again?"

"We will talk about it next week,"

"I will expect an answer." I hung up and thought about how easily motherhood could be silenced. Little did I know that I had only just begun to scratch the surface.

9
Suffering in Silence

Women die every day. It had never fully entered my consciousness until that first miscarriage. Potential mothers, mothers, grandmothers—all were vulnerable.

I had been given the approval from my obstetrician, Dr. Christine Barkley, to try again. I had a good feeling about things this time. I was in a good place, and I thought it was unlikely that I would have such bad luck twice in a row. I marveled at how the human brain could take statistics and twist and meld them in knots in order to spit out the answer that it wanted to hear. I was confident I was headed in the right direction.

As I headed out to my car, I heard my name being called in the background. At first, I thought I was hearing things, however the voice persisted and got progressively louder.

"Dr. Jones, Dr. Jones!"

I turned to see a somewhat familiar face. With so many patients and so many family members, faces were generally somewhat difficult to recognize. The look on my face must have reflected my confusion, as the owner of the voice began with a detailed description of who she was and why she was standing outside the hospital at 6:00

p.m. on a Friday night in November.

"Sylvia Root, I'm Sylvia Root. Justine's mother. You treated her for her cancer last year."

"Yes! I remember! How is she doing?"

"Better now. She came into hospital a week ago with what we thought was another bout of pneumonia. She is much better now, and we are hoping she will come home over the weekend. I am sure she would appreciate a visit from you!"

I hesitated for a moment and thought it would be nice to touch base with Justine, if only for a few minutes. I had been her surgeon last year, and it sounded as if she was in hospital for an unrelated condition. I was certain that I had seen her in follow up only six months ago and that everything had been fine, as far as remission from her cancer was concerned.

"Sure! Lead the way."

We proceeded back inside the large glass doors on the west side of the hospital, wound our way along the first floor and took the elevator to floor nine. We rode quietly, side by side. We turned left off the elevator and wandered down to the second to last room on the left-hand side. I was not familiar with this floor of the hospital.

"Look who I found in the parking lot!" exclaimed Justine's mother as we entered the private room. "Dr. Jones was just leaving the hospital when we had the good fortune to run into each another."

Again, the look on my face must have said it all. Lying before me was not someone who was just visiting the hospital with 'another case of uncomplicated pneumonia'. Justine must have been about half the size of her former robust self. Her eyes peered out at me from hollowed sockets and her pajamas hung loosely about her listless frame. When she rose to speak, it was as if she had to recruit every muscle fibre in her weary body just to sit up.

"Hello," Justine smiled. "It's nice to see you."

"I was just telling Dr. Jones that we expect you to make a full recovery and we expect you will be home over the weekend, if not shortly thereafter!"

Justine and I smiled at each other. As our eyes connected, I sensed that we both knew there was a secret between the two of us. It was often like that in patients with end-stage, terminal cancer.

"Mom, could I speak with Dr. Jones for a few minutes in private?"

"For sure! I know that you have a lot to catch up on. Don't forget to tell her about your plan to travel to Europe next summer. We are all so excited for you!" With that, she was gone.

I turned toward Justine. "I ... I can explain," she stammered. "I don't want to burden Mom. The cancer is back in my lungs. I tried an experimental drug. I don't want to take chemo because I don't want to be sick. They tell me I have six months to live. I am hoping for another year or two."

I stared at her in disbelief. I didn't know what to say.

"My family has no idea. I have asked the doctors to say nothing. I have told everyone I am losing a little weight and exercising more. It seems to be working."

Again, I didn't know what to say. I had dealt with many patients over the years who were fighting the ravages of cancer. I had never happened upon someone who appeared to be in the late stages of cancer and had concocted such an intricate and highly inaccurate story to protect those around them. She had hidden everything. I was at once amazed and angered.

"The doctors keep asking me what they should do if my heart or lungs stop. I have told them to do everything. They should never mention to my parents or family that the cancer is back. I know you are my friend. You can't breathe a word of this to anyone."

I had been asked only once previously to function as someone's friend and not their doctor. That did not end well for anyone, myself included. I found it difficult to envision how keeping this news from those closest to oneself was in anyone's best interest. Certainly, people around Justine either suspected, would begin to suspect or would be left to wonder after the fact, why they had missed the signs. I wondered if Justine's mother suspected nothing, as her words and actions would suggest, or whether she was choosing to participate in this intricate fable, unbeknownst to her daughter, in order to provide some comfort in her daughter's final days. I reminded myself that I had only stumbled upon the scenario not even an hour ago, and that I was not responsible for its inception or ongoing evolution. I explained that I would say nothing further, I wished her comfort and safety, and then I excused myself.

I was thankful that there was no one around as I made a mad dash down the elevator, out the doors of the hospital and into my car. I don't think that I took more than one breath during the entire two-minute flight.

Two weeks later, I read that Justine had passed away peacefully with her family by her side. Her obituary commented on 'her long battle with cancer' and 'her courageous spirit in the face of a difficult situation'. I knew that her mother knew everything and had always known everything. I knew her mother had been, and would continue to, suffer in silence like only a mother can.

10

A Victoria Jones Novel

I glanced over at the clock beside my bed—6:10 a.m.—and reflected on the confusing silence of the previous evening. Both of my children were at sleepovers with only one due back home today. It came rushing back to me that I had crafted a lofty goal, to unsilence motherhood, and that my number one strategy for doing this would be to write a novel. This would be an anthology of stories exploring the many ways in which the silence of motherhood deserved to be heard. I reminded myself that I should never combine good wine with being post call! It seemed that lofty ambitions stood in the wings waiting to soar in.

I got up, fed everyone left at home, including my three cats and the leopard gecko, Electron. I fought with the treadmill for half an hour. I reflected on whether it was too lofty a goal to tackle an entire novel at this point in my life, given that I was passionate about the subject matter. The kids were older, the surgeries that I commonly performed had become almost mechanistic and mundane, and it seemed as if the idea I had always been looking for to inspire a passion for writing was now right in front of me. It was virtually screaming for recognition.

"OK!" I said out loud. "You win!"

Before sitting down at my computer, I texted both my sons. I recognized that it was only 7:30 a.m. and that I was unlikely to get any kind of response for several more hours.

There were many stories that floated through my head. Some belonged to me and some belonged to others; all would be invaluable in making the point. There were many ways in which motherhood was silenced. From the belief that motherhood was natural or easy and therefore did not require much discussion; to the numerous ways that women and children were separated, whether alive or dead; and finally, to the loss that each mother feels when independence kicks down the sacred door of childhood. It was hardly ever given more than just a fleeting thought or a simple comment. There were those who meticulously chose the relationship and its timing, like myself, and those for whom it was unexpected, but exciting. Regardless of the path by which they got there, some mothers found it somewhat empty, while still others found that it put them in a position where it robbed them of parts of themselves or even the central essence of who they truly were or who they could become as a person. Further, it was hard for the world to accept that some women would never be able to think of themselves as mothers, whether they had children or not. My novel had to speak to all the various ways in which the mother-child relationship had never previously been explored and how it was needlessly silenced.

I decided that my life would be a good basis for many of the stories to be told and that other accounts would be anchored around the many women who had passed into, out of, and through my life. I believed that single mothers who intentionally chose to have children on their own experienced many forms of silence that affected their own sense of self and the mother-child relationship. Some of these would be experienced by other mothers in other circumstances. Some situations, such as the death or betrayal of a spouse, and how that would relate to the mother-child relationship, would be foreign to single mothers by choice like myself. I had often thought about what it might be like to have a partner who did not care that I existed and how that would colour my life and the relationships I might have with my children. I was thankful that I had been blessed with the ability to define myself and my relationships with my children on my own terms.

I knew starting with the title would be fruitless. I thought that I should have some form of outline but reminded myself this was a novel and not a term paper. God, how long had it been since I had even constructed a term paper; was it even called that anymore? I should start at the beginning, but what was the beginning? Was it the beginning in time or when the idea first tipped into a passionate existence? I wondered how anyone was ever able to pen a coherent novel when the possibilities were endless.

I decided to start with the passion and move on from there. The tipping point was the palpable silence from the previous evening with the departure of my two children at the same time. I harkened back and tried to re-harness the energy and emotion of that moment. Things were different in the night, more emotional and intense. I closed my eyes and leaned back to try to recreate the moment.

Four hours later, I had created and recreated the

opening paragraph of my novel. Logan had come in, eaten a hearty breakfast of pancakes, eggs and bacon, and left again. I had answered several emails and texts from family and friends and checked in to make sure my patients were all doing well. I was alone again, but I could not recreate the intense sense of loss that Silence had ushered in the previous evening during his visit.

At 2:00 p.m., Logan texted to ask if he could have another sleepover. I called him excitedly to say that another sleepover would be more than fabulous! From the sound of his voice, I could tell that my excitement had caught him slightly off guard. I was not usually so excited to hear that my children were leaving me alone for the evening. I could now sit back and wait for Silence to consume my house as night loomed in the background.

At 7:00 p.m., I put on some of my favorite jazz music and started pacing the floors. I knew this place so well, as well as I am sure it knew me. I could see my children at various stages of their lives, in various rooms of the house. The good times, the bad times, the hard times; they were all there waiting for me to unravel once again. As I turned the corner into the front hallway, pictures of my children at a very young age came into my view. There it was, the feeling from the previous evening hit me square in the heart. The silence of motherhood raised its head once again.

I sat down at my computer and began to grapple with the opening paragraph once again. It had to capture the reader, as they say. After at least a dozen further attempts, I knew I had hit upon something that would show the passion of the author.

The Silence of Motherhood

The loud silence that enveloped my house was foreign to the story of our lives. This was not a place where I ever expected that I would be, although I had longed for it endlessly, especially in those early days. I had longed for it, and now I did not want it. In fact, I loathed it. How could my perfect life be disrupted by what I thought that I had always wanted? I could hear it echoing in from the corners of my mind, in a voice which was all too familiar, that of my best friend Rosalee Crookman, 'Be careful what you wish for, Tori!'

I looked up at the clock—10:00 p.m. I texted both my children, knowing full well that I would be on the bottom of the list of the things that they would be interested in this evening. Oh well, at least I had the mother of the year award tucked away high in my closet, safe from the rest of the world. With that knowledge, and the pride of having written a single paragraph, I closed my computer for the evening. As they say, each novel begins with a single paragraph.

11

Self insemination

One month after Justine's death, I was in Dr. Barkley's office waiting for the next chapter of my life to unfold. As I lay on the cold table, looking up at the stark lifeless ceiling, I drifted in and out of awareness as I followed my favorite meditation app with my ears and my mind. Meditation, like Silence, was a close friend. I think it was because the three of us had similar interests—do a good job and move on.

It was obvious that Christine, Dr. Barkley to the outside world, was in somewhat of a rush that day. I thanked her for fitting me in at the end of a long, busy day. She again expressed her condolences on the loss of my first pregnancy. I reflected for a moment that it had not actually been my first pregnancy, however I forced that thought to the back of my mind. I stated that I had moved on and was ready to take the plunge for the second time. I understood that there were risks, as there is with almost anything in life. There is no success without real risk.

As she inserted the frigid speculum, I laughed and commented that this would be much easier with some fine wine, soft candlelight and Mr. Right—or even Mr.

Right Now! We made idle chit-chat about our jobs and the dedication it took to be successful in our respective fields. Aside from the speculum, I noted no specific feeling as she deftly and efficiently performed the insemination. I marveled at how quick and seamless the potential creation of a new life could be. We both laughed as she got up, not even three minutes later, and asked that I remain lying for about five minutes before I got up to leave.

"You can show yourself out, I assume?"

"Certainly! Thanks!" With that, she was gone.

I looked up at the ceiling once again and said out loud, "Well, that is that." How simple it seemed. I had read countless stories of women spending thousands of dollars on appointments, tests and prescriptions in search of the elusive highly desired pregnancy. I had spent twenty minutes choosing the donor and called my obstetrician when I was ovulating. It doesn't get much easier than that. I had a good feeling about things this time!

As I watched the clock on the wall approach five minutes, I wondered who was coming back to remove the speculum. I thought I remembered waiting five minutes the last time I had been in this precarious position, but I did not remember having to personally deal with the speculum. I was sure that I had been in many, many much more difficult situations before, but right at the present moment my mind was drawing an elusive blank. As a physician, I had even used a speculum on numerous occasions myself, in a professional capacity. I rolled my eyes and thought about what kind of bizarre contortionist movements I was going to have to engage in, the end goal being to get the speculum out while leaving the desired contents inside.

I certainly hoped that the 'swimmers' of the day were moving as quickly as their qualifying spreadsheet boasted they could, toward their desired destination.

I decided that I was going to wait five minutes more and then I was going to make my move. I felt that five minutes would leave me enough time to google 'freeing oneself from an unwanted speculum' or 'five easy steps to self-insemination'. If all else failed, I was going to admit defeat and call the front desk. While some interesting, and I am sure invaluable, information arose from these two searches, including 'how to free yourself from a manipulator', 'how to free yourself from love that hurts, and 'how to inseminate at home', there was nothing that informed me on how I could free myself from my present predicament.

I called the front desk and was disheartened when my important inquiry went through to voicemail informing me that the clinic was closed until tomorrow morning. I patted my abdomen and muttered 'well kid, I guess it's just you and me now'.

It had now been twenty-seven minutes since Christine's departure. I decided that was long enough. I tilted my pelvis up and placed a pillow underneath my butt. I unscrewed the speculum in the direction that I thought was correct—backwards like steering a boat. I counted to three, tilted my pelvis up and removed the speculum. What talent! Sometimes I even impressed myself!

I quickly dressed and opened the door to almost complete darkness. I had forgotten how quickly the night descends during the winter solstice. I grabbed my coat and ran directly for the front door. I was travelling too quickly to notice the red warning sign sitting atop the door, and as soon as the cold night air rushed in, a sound louder than I thought I had ever heard before was unleashed from the clinic. Even when the door slammed shut behind me, the alarm persisted in trying to escape. I debated making a run for it or simply remaining where I was and awaiting my destiny. The decision was made for me. It was too late.

12
You Can't Make This Stuff Up!

I had tried to explain to the first two officers that had shown up on the scene that I was a patient of Dr. Barkley's and that I had been left in the clinic after hours to fend for myself. I did not think that detailing the successful manipulations that I had made to extract myself from inside the clinic would add much, besides embarrassment, to the conversation. I explained that I had been locked in the clinic after hours, and that when I had tried to let myself out the alarm system had been triggered. I went on to explain that I myself was a physician. They were having none of it. I would be escorted down to the station while they waited for Dr. Barkley to return their call. Apparently, she was not on call and the switchboard had no way of reaching her.

When we reached the station, I was placed directly into the interrogation room. Another officer, one whom I did not recognize from the six that eventually showed up at the scene, entered and sat across from me. She did not appear to be very happy that I had disrupted her otherwise uneventful evening.

"I am Officer Smith, Cindy Smith. It would be best

if you were as truthful as possible about the events of the evening."

"I'll do my best."

"Please run me through the events from the time that you entered the clinic this afternoon until the alarm went off."

"Well ...," I stammered. "Dr. Barkley is my obstetrician. I was having an insemination done this afternoon, and she accidently left the speculum in. She instructed me to wait five minutes, however when no one returned to remove the speculum, I had to figure out how to do that myself." The look on her face was a mix of disgust, disbelief and amusement. "I was trying to google how to get out of this situation. By the time I recognized that the Internet was not going to provide me with any useful information, I decided to call the front desk of the clinic. My call went straight to voicemail, and I recognized that the clinic was closed and everyone had left. I released myself from the speculum, no small feat I might add, and quickly dressed and went for the door. I did not recognize that it was an emergency exit. The alarm signaled my exit and that is how I first met your partners." I decided that trying to sugar coat this would be of no benefit. I was also relieved that she was a female, and I was unlikely to have to go into a more detailed description of the use of a speculum.

The look on her face was one which I interpreted as a combination of shock, humour and anger. I was looking for a little commiseration but could find none.

"I see," she said, barely able to contain what I thought was hopefully laughter. "I find it hard to believe that the doctor would forget to do something she does many times a day. It's probably a reflex."

"I don't think I could make this stuff up!"

"There have been five separate attempts to steal supplies and medications from clinics in the Calgary region over the last month. We must follow all leads. This seems like a rather strong one. I don't care if you are a physician. You are still a suspect!"

"Perhaps, except I did not do anything or steal anything. If you allow me to call Dr. Barkley on her cell phone, I am sure we can clear this whole thing up."

"We have called her cell phone. She is not answering."

"What about the receptionist from the clinic? She will have my name in the appointment calendar."

"How would we contact her?"

"Please allow me to call Dr. Saunders. He shares the clinic with Dr. Barkley. I am sure we can get all the information that you need from him."

She allowed me to call Dr. Greg Saunders through the operator at the main hospital. I thought it was quite humorous that the switchboard clerk asked me how my night was going when I asked her to put me through to Greg.

"Greg, it's Tori Jones."

"Great to hear from you! What's up?"

As I relayed the story to him, I could tell that he could barely contain himself. He asked to be put on the line with the officer in charge. After a brief discussion, Officer Smith hung up the receiver, picked it up again and dialed.

"Hello, is this Samantha Viceroy who works at the Blueline Obstetrics Clinic on Westerly Street?" Dr. Smith asked. I assumed it was an affirmative as she continued.

"This is Officer Cindy Smith from the downtown precinct. We have a lady here, a Dr. Victoria Jones. She claims she is a patient of Dr. Barkley's and that she got left alone in the clinic. Can you confirm she was a patient today?" She went on to relay more of the story. My God, how many would need to know?

Officer Smith was silent for about thirty seconds. "Thank you for your time. I will relay your apologies to the doctor."

"You are free to go. We are sorry for taking your time. We need to follow every lead."

I didn't know what to say. I was tired, hungry and just happy that things had finally been settled this evening. I had been imagining spending the night in the slammer with people accused of crimes much more heinous than mine.

"Good luck," she exclaimed. "Maybe this will bring you luck."

I thought it was a strange way to end the evening, however I decided to go with it.

13
What is Fiction?

Sunday morning, I awoke at 6:30 a.m. and headed downstairs to make myself a large, steaming mug of hot chocolate with marshmallows. I curled up in my favorite chair, with my favorite blanket, and hoped that I could take in a good movie before my children finally arrived home for the day. I flipped studiously through Netflix, finally settling upon one of my favorites, *Aliens*. I always marveled that it was one of the few movies where the sequel was better than the original. As I made myself comfortable, I assumed that the cats would be arriving shortly. My mind wandered, as the movie unraveled in front of me, as to how I would deal with an unstable trauma patient who came into the emergency room after having had an alien rip itself into life from the center of their unsuspecting body. I envisioned controlling the hemorrhage, repairing the heart and trying to pull everything back together in a race against time. It would be a fascinating adventure in human anatomy and a challenge that I always thought that I could successfully rise to.

I was feeling immensely impressed with myself that I had managed to crank out a single opening paragraph during the late hours of the previous evening. At that rate, I would have the novel completed in about three years, if not longer! I was going to have to speed up the process considerably. I promised myself that I was going to dedicate at least an hour a day to the writing process, between my job as a full-time surgeon and a full-time mother. "After all," I said to myself, "this is now your passion."

My younger son, Lucas, arrived just as I was marveling once again on the grit and resilience of Sigourney Weaver as a woman who repeatedly defends herself and others against the tireless aliens. Not surprisingly, the movie always ended in the same way—an unrelenting battle between two fierce women, one trying to potentiate her species and one trying to eradicate the other. It was anyone's guess as to who was playing which role. In my mind, each woman was playing both roles. I was reflecting on the complex and vicious nature of disagreements between the females of any species, human or otherwise, when Lucas came around the corner. I smiled at the sight of his blond hair and piercing blue eyes. He smiled back at me revealing purple and orange elastics braided through his silver braces.

"Hi, Mom! How are you doing? I have missed you!"

"Well! How was your weekend away from your loving mother?"

"Great! We played lots of video games. Jeremy's dad took us to play Laser tag with a bunch of other guys. Lots of good food!"

My youngest was always about the food, very much different than my oldest, Logan. I could always expect a great description of what had been eaten, which I found very satisfying and entertaining. He truly took after me in this regard.

"We had stuffed pizza on Friday night—to die for—cheese and pepperoni!" He exclaimed, licking his lips and rubbing his upper abdomen. "We had Ben and Jerry's Cookie Dough ice cream for dessert. Then yesterday we had French toast for breakfast, burgers for lunch and a great stir fry for dinner." He continued to lick his lips as he seemed to be vividly reliving each meal.

He came over to where I was sitting and gave me a big hug. "I'm going up to my room."

"Already? Come and sit by your old mom for a few minutes and let's talk about what we are going to do today. I thought we might go bowling."

"All right," he replied somewhat reluctantly. "I was hoping to spend some time in my room."

"Sounds like you! I was planning a vacation for this summer with about forty of your half brothers and sisters. We are doing an all-inclusive in Mexico. Remember the last time we went? You and your brother had a great time swimming with the dolphins, and I really loved the lazy river."

"Yes! The sibs are always a good time! I remember that great Disney vacay. We travelled as a pack! I was hoping to go on another trip."

We talked for a few minutes about some of the fond memories that we both had from excursions with the 'sibs' as he liked to call them. Our first trip had been to a large cottage complex in the Hamptons about seven years ago. There were about ten of the known thirty half brothers and sisters, ranging in age from about three to nine, who had attended this first meeting. We had become acquainted through the Donor Sibling Registry website, which sought to acquaint donor offspring with those related to them, in our case by sperm donation. I had communicated with people who had used the same donor for several years before taking the plunge to meet in person. I had never looked back.

Neither had my older son, Logan, who seemed to have formed a strong and enduring connection with many of his half-siblings. He kept in constant contact with them by way of Snapchat and Instagram. Since that first vacation, we had managed to get away with some of the sibs and their families about once or twice a year. It was always amazing to me how similar the siblings were. There were similar physical features and mannerisms that a majority of the siblings seemed to have. All the parents were constantly looking for common traits, especially following the research that had come out several years ago with respect to a number of children from a common sperm donor who were found to be on the autism spectrum. I tried not to take it too seriously, aside from my insistence that 'good' traits were always likely passed down through my side of the family. I took full credit for my children's good looks, fabulous brains and overall greatness!

I was excited that we were heading back to Mexico. It was good for the kids to be able to have some freedom and for the adults to get to know each other better over a few exotic cocktails. These were always good times for everyone involved!

There had not been as many questions from the children recently, as there had been in the past, about the path to their existence. They knew they had a sperm donor, and they knew the logistics of how that worked, but my children were more concerned with relational issues between themselves and the donor. How could they find the donor, what would the donor's reaction be, and where would that fit into their busy lives? Sometimes, I wished I could help them more by understanding their desperation and by being enough as a single parent. It never seemed as if it was enough, even though there was far less chaos in our household then there had been when I was growing up. I often wished that one of my parents would leave. If one of them were to have left, at least there would have been more time for me to spend with my good friend Silence. I remembered how many times I asked my mother why there could not just be more calmness in our lives. I guess every kid yearns for what they cannot have.

"Can I go now? I have things to do."

"Well, if you have *things to do*, by all means don't let me keep you. He gave me a big hug and left.

About ten minutes later, Logan walked in. The movie had ended, and I was just in the process of patting myself on the back for having successfully resuscitated another victim of an alien birth.

"Hi, Mom! How was your weekend?" He came over and sat down on the couch beside me. I thought about how different my children were and how I never had to ask my older son to sit with me. He just naturally navigated his 6'4" slender frame over to me. I was constantly on the lookout for those small signals that would harken the shift into an unrecognizable teenage monster. Luckily, there had been no discernable sign of this.

"Good! Good, but lonely." I joked as I lovingly slapped him on the knee.

"Sorry, I thought I should probably have said no to the second night of the sleepover because you would be alone again."

"No problem!" I often wondered how difficult it was to be the oldest child of a single parent. There was really no opportunity to ever be a child. There was always the worry about your mother and what your role in the family was. I thought this must be especially difficult for boys who would expect themselves to be the 'man of the family'.

"I enjoyed the time with Silence, as you know I always do," I lied. "It is nice to have some time to myself. I also decided that I am going to write a novel."

"Interesting, what about?" It was funny how both my children were always somewhat nonchalant when I announced I was going to embark on another significant adventure. I imagined that one day I would assert that I was going to be travelling to Mars or that I was going to have a third arm attached to my body, and they would both reply 'Interesting, when will that happen?'.

"I haven't quite decided yet. Probably a work of fiction."

"Is fiction the true or the fake one? I can't remember."

"The fake one."

"Good, then I will be safe," he said, walking away from me and into the kitchen where I could hear the fridge door open.

I did not reply, and he did not inquire further.

14
Breaking the Silence

I was in my second trimester of a very easy and uncomplicated pregnancy when I decided to speak with my boss, Dr. Christias, about my exciting situation. It had been almost two uneventful weeks since the results of the CVS had returned showing a normal male fetus. This had resulted in an interesting, and somewhat unnerving, discussion with several of my closest friends as I had been convinced that any children I might have would be female. I had done some very deep soul searching as to why I thought as I did, given that my life was going to turn out much differently than I had anticipated. Having come from a long line of matriarchs, I guess I had just assumed that any child that was going to be strong enough to exist in this world, with a single parent, would need to be female. My friends of course found this all quite amusing.

I had no preconceived ideas about motherhood in general, and no preference for one sex over the other, however I had always imagined that my first child would be a daughter. Perhaps it was because I was the eldest. I was uncertain as to how a male child would survive the ravages of the current world if something were to happen to me. I knew women could be strong, but what about men? My good friends, all of them strong women of one sort or another, continued to remind me, almost daily, of the hilarity of the situation. They all knew that I was in for the ride of my life!

I had always had a good relationship with my Department Chair. He knew my passion for the profession of surgery and that I was dedicated to transferring my knowledge of the discipline to the next generation. I was not nervous about our discussion, I just wanted to make sure he was aware that I did not want to be the perfect mother and the perfect surgeon, I just wanted to be good at both.

It was a bleak Wednesday afternoon after I had finished in the OR. I had just closed on a very difficult case in Theatre 20 where the patient had nearly passed away on the operating room table. It was not my case; I was pulled in to assist by one of my junior colleagues. We had spent the better part of the last several hours saving the patient; saving her from hemorrhaging to death and from the long slow deterioration that she would be committed to if we could not remove all of the tumour. We had been successful on both counts. *Mostly luck,* I thought. It was best to think this way as Surgery was not a kind mentor. The more you thought that you were able to perform miracles, the more likely the results of your efforts would end in travesty. At least this is what I had always told myself.

I was unsure if I should keep my appointment with Dr. Christias. Although I had a good relationship with him, I was way beyond fatigued. I had spent most of my pregnancy this way, and after the ordeal that I had just been through with a patient who had been trying to die on me for the last two hours, and who was not yet out of the woods, I felt more like I should just put my head down on my desk and cry. As Dr. Christias' office was just across from mine, I decided not to delay the inevitable.

I knocked on the door. A familiar voice replied, "Come in."

I turned the handle and opened the door to Dr. Ben Christias sitting at his desk. I guessed that he was about fifty-five with greying temples peppering his blondish hair. He wore blue issue scrubs covered by a crisp white lab coat emblazoned with his name in black letters across the right breast pocket. His brown eyes always seemed somewhat sad. He was of average height and build, with no defining marks, scars or tattoos. I knew that the latter probably went without saying, however I had recently read an article that claimed that over forty per cent of adults admitted to some type of identifying body art. I had estimated this to be about zero per cent in surgeons older than the age of fifty. It was certainly something I wanted to know nothing further about!

There were piles of charts and papers everywhere. Ben looked very weary. I thought that the number of charts and files littering his office had significantly increased since the last time I had been there less than two months earlier. I did not understand how he could possibly tolerate the clutter or find anything he needed for that matter. I knew that I would not be able to tolerate this kind of random collection of things lying about if it were my office. "If you are busy I could come back another time," I said, not really wanting to enter now that I had almost crossed the threshold.

"No! I am expecting you to take me away from my misery for a few minutes. I have piles of charts to dictate and apparently no energy to attend to this godforsaken task. How are you doing on this fine day?"

"Fine! You?"

"Can't complain. Wouldn't do me any good even if I did!"

We both laughed, and I sat down in the only chair that was void of paperwork. It seemed as if every time I came into his office there was more and more stuff. His degrees were displayed elegantly on one wall, and several framed pictures detailing the history of Calgary dating back to 1950, faced off against these on the opposite wall. There was a framed oil depicting the Kananaskis Rocky Mountains hanging just above his head. A full length unframed mirror resided on the back of the door. A large Stickley mission style desk was opposite the door. Next to the desk was a clothes rack with several pairs of blues, which appeared to have been crumpled up and thrown, rather than placed, onto the hooks. If this were basketball tryouts, rather than the Department of Surgery, my boss would be a superstar!

"What can I do you for?" He laid his pen down on his desk and quietly closed his laptop, one of two LED screens on his desk. He turned and diverted his full attention towards me.

"I wanted to speak with you about something on a more personal level; something that will likely impact the surgical schedule and my path for promotion over the next several years."

"Are you unwell?"

"Not ... really ..." I stammered.

"Well, if you are not sick, I am sure that whatever you are going to tell me will be positive, I hope?"

That was just like Ben. Always looking for the golden side of everything.

"I'm pregnant! About three months."

There was a moment of silence. By the look on his face, I could tell that Ben had been caught off guard by my revelation. It seemed like an eternity before he finally voiced his response, and during that time I wondered whether this had been the wrong time and the wrong place to expose this extremely sensitive information. I was brought back to reality by his response.

"Well, that is wonderful news! I definitely was not expecting that. We will need to have some discussion about what we can do to support you with this."

I appreciated his comments. I had already been thinking, for years, about how this was going to unravel—from before the first time I had attended a Single Mothers by Choice session in New York City, which was for women who were just thinking about having a child on their own. I had a well-developed plan for all aspects of this child's life, all aspects that I had anticipated, that is. However, I appreciated that I might not have thought of everything. Perhaps, I had not thought of anything that was truly important, for that matter.

"Thank you," I exhaled. "I am pretty sure that I have thought of almost everything, but one never knows. I am dedicated to being a great surgeon and to being a great parent. That, I am definitely sure of! I probably will need to make some of it up as I go along, but I will cross that bridge when I come to it."

I was used to 'making things up as I went along'. I think that any woman who works in a highly male dominated field, even in this 'age of equality', is used to that. I was more fortunate than some of the women in the stories that had been relayed to me in the past; stories of harassment and condescension that were often avidly swept under the rug. I knew that the greatest threat to the progress of women in a career like mine was not admitting when there was a problem, upholding the myth of equality, and smiling through the whole process. Ben knew that I was always very upfront about my view of the struggles of women and the subtle ways in which these struggles reared their nasty heads. He recognized the inherent biases of academic medicine in bolstering the careers of those moving along the traditional trajectory, mostly men, and how the efforts of women sometimes went without the same outpouring of recognition. I was impressed by the continued genuine attempts he had made in an effort to remedy the situation, not by demanding that I 'suck it up and conform' like some of my past senior acquaintances had. His style was to let a person's strengths shine through, especially when their strengths are off the beaten track. For me, that was the type of thing that was needed to let my career and my personal life flourish.

"I know you will let me know, in no uncertain terms, what you need!" He knew me too well.

"Great! Let's just keep this between you and me for now." I left his office and closed the door, not knowing exactly what I meant by that. Keeping things to myself was not a luxury that was going to be available to me much longer!

15
Surgeon or Mother?

The 'keeping this between you and me' statement did not last long. By my sixth month, I began to wonder if I was ever going to be known, in professional circles, as simply Dr. Victoria Jones ever again. My venture into motherhood seemed to come with many unexpected benefits! There always seemed to be nutritious snacks that miraculously appeared in my clinic, a fabulous footrest in the operating theatre, and lots of offers for juice and other liquid refreshments while I was operating. There was an unending supply of everything that I seemed to want or crave. Interestingly, I seemed to have a craving for orange food, not orange flavored food, but foods of an orange color. Some of my favorites were cheddar cheese and papayas—sometimes separately and sometimes combined—depending on the day!

I was lucky that I felt well and that my life seemed to be progressing along virtually unscathed. None of the other surgeons seemed to notice that anything was different, or if they did, no one was saying anything. I was not sure what that meant, and I saw it as a somewhat unnerving silence. I reflected back on my initial disclosure to my boss, Ben Christias, some months previously. He knew that I would make him aware of any issues, however it did not seem like there was any cause for concern. I had heard many stories from my female colleagues about discrimination or harassment, which seemed to be accentuated when they became pregnant, I had experienced none of this. I believed that it was not because I had chosen to turn a blind eye. When it came to gender-related issues, I was like a vulture. I was always hovering and waiting for my next unknowing prey to fall victim to my oft-rehearsed diatribes with respect to the 'weaker sex'. Weaker sex, my ass!

And then it happened ...

I was sitting in the Doctor's Lounge waiting to scrub for a complex case involving a large, recurrent tumour of the abdomen. The patient had signed over their future to myself and two of my colleagues who were known for stepping up to the plate when no one else was willing to. I could not even begin to count how many of this type of operation I had performed previously. I was sure it was greater than 100. To the unfamiliar eye, 100 might seem like a small number, but given the uncommon nature of this tumour and the even more uncommon need for this type of surgery, I was considered to be an expert in my field.

The operation involved the removal of several organs and most of the tailbone. It was an operation that generally took my team between six and twelve hours. It involved four different operating teams. For as long as I could remember, I had been the person who had orchestrated the team towards success, both inside and outside the operating suite. We walked patients through a complex operation, with the potential for death and other significant complications including blood loss, and then confined them to hospital for anywhere between one and four weeks, sometimes longer. We left them with two bags, one to collect urine and one to collect stool. In men, we rendered them impotent. The physical and psychological effects were nothing short of significant. All of this was done with an intent to cure patients, but with no specific guarantee that the tumour would not return, sometimes with a vengeance, in a very short period of time.

The newest member of the team, Dr. Reynolds Ross, had trained as a cancer urologist. He had been hired about a year ago, and I had invited him along as a favour to Dr. Jim Jonas, a good friend and skilled colleague who usually worked alongside me in cases such as this. Reynolds had been present at less than a handful of these types of procedures during the time I had known him, and always under the close supervision of Dr. Jonas. It was always exciting to think that we were developing future surgeons who would be successful in this area. Reynolds would be responsible for taking the lead on removal of the bladder and creation of the urine bag.

Reynolds entered into the Doctor's Lounge and walked directly over to me. He asked how I was doing and when I was off for maternity leave. It was the most any of my colleagues, besides my Chair, had inquired about my condition since it had become apparent what was unfolding.

"I am doing great! I am off on maternity leave for about three months starting in about six weeks. I am concerned that I might get bored during my time off."

"Great! Listen, I have taken the liberty of inviting your colleague, Dr. Gordon, to assist us in the OR today. I knew that you would likely be off soon, and I did not want the patient to be caught on the short end of the stick without their surgeon to follow them up. You can take the day off! Maybe go to the spa."

I couldn't even process what was being said to me, at me. I, Dr. Victoria Jones, was being asked, no told, that I was being excused from my own case, a case that I was the primary referral for and one that I had done all the work to co-ordinate. I was the named surgeon on the OR slate, and I was being told by this junior colleague that I was being excused because I was a woman and because I was having a child!

"I am sorry! I don't believe I heard you correctly. I am the primary surgeon for this case, and I have every intention of being in the room when the patient is being operated on. You have no right to go behind my back and arrange for alternate care. I have never heard of anything as outrageous as what you are suggesting to me!"

Without even blinking, he continued. "I believe I have every right to ensure that patients receive the best care possible, from the best team. The team has to be able to provide continuous care to the patient. This is something that you will not be able to do. Why make this any harder on yourself than it has to be?"

This was going from bad to worse. I looked around the room and thought that this all felt very surreal. These were the type of things that I had only heard of.

And now it was happening ...

Someone laid their hand on my right shoulder and

shook me as if trying to awaken me. I must have jumped, as I turned toward Dr. Christias who looked somewhat startled.

"Dr. Jones, I was wondering how you are doing. You seem like you are off somewhere in deep thought. Is there something going on?"

I harkened back to the meeting in his office when I had first told him of my pregnancy. He asked me to come to him with anything that I needed. In the moment, however, I couldn't even comprehend how he was going to be able to assist in the situation. As I turned my head to the right, I noticed that Dr. Ross, Reynolds, was still standing there.

"Nothing, I need to get to the OR. My patient needs me!" I shot a nasty look in the direction of Dr. Ross.

As I entered the room, I noticed that my junior colleague, Dr. Gordon, was already there.

"Good morning!" He exclaimed. "I am so excited that you asked me to be the primary assistant along with Dr. Ross and the others on this case. I have been waiting for an opportunity like this!"

What a façade! I wasn't even aware that this was an area of interest for Dr. Gordon, Michael as I referred to him. This was a very complex operation and the General Surgical Oncologist was always the co-ordinator of the case. I was unsure as to whether Michael was ready to step up to that role.

"Michael, can I speak with you in private?" I asked.

"Great!"

As we walked into the scrub area, I thought about how I was going to address this. I knew Michael as a very good surgeon from when he was a resident. He was technically very good and had excellent judgement. I was not sure how he had even gotten this far into this case without there being some form of communication between the two of us. I reminded myself that I needed to be direct, without emotion, and I needed to keep in mind that the goal was the safe orchestration of the procedure that was about to unfold in front of us over the next many hours.

"I was not aware that this type of case was something that you were interested in. I have not seen you in attendance at any of these types of cases as a resident or even in the first several years of your practice. Why did you not involve me in the discussion? Why did you not seek me out to review your approach?" I practically had to tape my own mouth shut to refrain from the further onslaught of questions I wanted to hurl in his general direction.

"Dr. Ross ... told me ... um, that I would be doing you a favour," he stammered.

"Go on."

"He told me that I would be doing you a favour by stepping up to the plate. The way he presented it, I thought that you and he had discussed this. It seems as if I might be wrong."

"Do you feel prepared to be the primary operator?"

"Yes, I have been preparing for several weeks and ..."

"Several weeks! How long ago did Dr. Ross approach you about this?"

"I don't know, about four weeks ago, I suppose."

I reflected on where we should go from here. There was a patient who needed us, who was depending on us, already present in the operating room and awaiting my word on what we were going to do. I had taken the liberty of speaking with Dr. Smith, the anaesthesiologist, before taking Michael aside. I had asked him to give me a few minutes to get the team together to review our approach. This was, fortunately, not an uncommon request in cases such as this.

"All right," I replied. "You may take the lead, but I will remain in the room for the entire case. I will be scrubbed, and I will take the liberty of taking over whenever I feel it is necessary. The whole team will be aware that this is how things will be going down." I could not believe that I had just used such inappropriate phraseology.

"I ... I ... am sorry for my role in this," Michael responded. "I would like to proceed, and I am all right with you taking over at any time. I respect you and would never have gone behind your back on this."

I decided to let it drop. I needed Michael to be calm if he were going to proceed as planned.

We re-entered the operating theatre. After comforting the patient as he went off to sleep, I explained to the whole team, Dr. Ross included, how things were going to proceed. I could feel him wince as I outlined everyone's roles in what we were about to orchestrate. I finished my explanation, completed the time out and went out to the scrub sink where I had prepared for this very case so many times before. I scrubbed and took my seat off to the side of where the main action was going to take place.

Several hours later, things were progressing well, but slowly. I had been asked for advice a few times and had assisted in guiding the team to where they needed to go. I unscrubbed and stepped out for a few minutes as I had done many times in the past while allowing senior residents a few minutes to proceed on their own.

I don't think I had been out of the room more than a few minutes when I was urgently paged. "Dr. Jones, 25, Operating Theatre 14. Dr. Jones, 25, Operating Theatre 14," the overhead paging system blared to anyone in the hospital who was willing to listen.

I briskly reapplied my face mask and entered the room. There appeared to be a lot of hemorrhage and Michael and Reynolds were attempting to stop the bleeding from deep within the pelvis of the patient's open abdomen.

"Dr. Gordon!" I blared. "What is the first rule of uncontrolled bleeding in the pelvis?"

"Packing," both Reynolds and Michael responded in unison.

"Well then, what are you waiting for?"

As they moved toward packing, I went to the head of the bed to speak with Dr. Smith. They were behind on resuscitation and needed some time to catch up. I instructed everyone that we were packing the pelvis, and we were going to wait to proceed until the patient had been stabilized. I asked if there were any questions, looking very pointedly back and forth between Michael and Reynolds. Hearing none, I went to scrub.

And that was how it happened …

16
And There It Was!

The rest of the operation proceeded without incident. I was always amazed at how time seemed to stand still when I was in a case such as this. The orthopedic surgeons came in to assist with removal of the tailbone. The intact specimen, including the patient's rectum, anus, bladder and tailbone was handed off to the pathologist to be examined over the next several weeks. The plastic surgeons came in to harvest the flap of skin, fat and muscle from the patient's belly, which would fill the large hole we had created. The operation, which had started at about 8:00 a.m., was almost complete as we edged toward 8:00 p.m. This had taken us longer than usual; however, I was happy that we had performed an adequate cancer operation and that the reconstruction, including both stomas, one for urine and one for stool, was successful.

Once the patient was deemed to be stable, I unscrubbed and went to speak with the family. I explained that everything was fine and that we had done what we intended to do. I outlined that because of the length of the operation, it was likely that the breathing tube may stay in at least overnight. I repeated to the family something I had told numerous families over my years as a surgeon—we would take it one day at a time.

I was totally exhausted and just wanted to be at home eating anything orange coloured. I thought that tonight would definitely be a cheddar cheese and papaya night. As I walked toward the change room, I could not believe my eyes. There was Dr. Ross approaching me, and he looked as if he had intentionally found me and was wanting to speak with me.

"Dr. Jones, I was wondering if I might have a word with you."

I turned and faced him directly head on. "We have both had a long day. In case you have not noticed, I am in the advanced stages of pregnancy, and I must get home and care for myself. Surely, someone like yourself must understand that?"

"Yes," he replied sheepishly.

With that I walked away.

And there it was, I thought.

I smiled silently.

17
The Death of Motherhood

The house was almost ready for another being. I loved how it reflected who I was, including the room that Logan was coming home to. I had fallen in love with the name the first time I had heard it. I also liked that it was unisex.

I walked around the house and admired my artwork. I had a love for the abstract and the colourful, especially as it related to my favorite season—autumn. There were what seemed like endless yellows and reds and oranges. These fearless colours were a great match for the dark woods and the simple colours that lined the walls of my house. I reflected on how many times I had walked through the halls and rooms of my house, with Silence, and contemplated the completion of another stage in my life.

I stopped at the full-length mirror in my front foyer. I turned to admire my reflection in profile. My blonde hair, which now fell straight only to my shoulders, was accompanied by full bangs. My face had gone from slender to round, representing the advanced stages of pregnancy. I wore a black velvet maternity shirt and blue jeans with an expandable waist band. I lamented that I was only able to wear orthopedic shoes but noted that the shiny black hue of my leather Danskin Crocs did not detract from the overall elegance of my outfit. I rubbed my expanding belly with my right hand, looking up to admire the colourful artwork in my foyer.

I was awakened from my daydreaming by the loud, interfering sound of my pager. I glanced down at the all too familiar number, the emergency room of the hospital I was on call for that evening. I wondered what excitement lay ahead at the other end of my pager. I set down my glass of water, a liquid that I had become very intimately reacquainted with since the start of my pregnancy, picked up my cell phone, and dialed the number with ease.

"Hello, this is Dr. Jones. Is someone looking for me?"

"Just a moment," instructed the voice on the other end of the line. "Your senior resident asked us to put you through to the intensive care unit."

"Dr. Jones?" the familiar voice of my favourite senior resident, Robert, came on the line.

"What is going on?"

"I wanted to give you the heads up about a patient in bed 14 in the ICU. She is a thirty-two-year-old female who seems to be having a significant upper GI bleed. She has active, ongoing bleeding. Her blood pressure is $^{80}/_{40}$ with a pulse rate of 130. She is still speaking with us, but she has been brought here for ongoing evaluation."

"Ok, why don't you get her set up for a scope and let me know what it shows." I was confident in Robert's ability to resuscitate the patient and provide me with a logical treatment plan for the patient. I was not covering endoscopy this evening, even though it was a large part of my practice. "I am on my way in. I am close enough that I will likely even catch the endoscopy. Do you think we will need to intubate the patient to scope her? We had better get consent for the scope and the possible OR all at the same time." I recognized this was a lot to ask all in one breath, however it was not an uncommon situation for a senior surgical resident to manage.

"She was transferred in from an outside hospital where she was admitted yesterday with an upper GI bleed. The bleeding seemed to stop spontaneously with minimal resuscitation and an octreotide infusion. There was an upper endoscopy performed, which showed diffuse gastritis with no specific area of more aggressive bleeding. I think she is too unstable for another scope outside of the operating room. I think she needs to be consented, taken to the operating room and scoped, with the proviso that she may need a partial or total gastrectomy if we cannot stop the bleeding."

"How much blood has she received?"

"That's the issue. She is a card-carrying Jehovah's Witness, confirmed by herself and her family. She and her husband both vehemently refuse any type of blood products. Her last hemoglobin was 97."

It would be very difficult to remove part or all of her stomach in the face of active blood loss without the use of blood products. I had been in situations where patients who were Jehovah's Witness required larger operations. We had been able to prepare for these circumstances, including preservation of the patient's own blood just prior to the operation. It would appear I would not be afforded any such luxury at this time.

"I am on my way in. Please speak with ethics to see if

there is anything else we should consider. Ask hematology if they have anything to add. I also think that you should reiterate to the patient and her husband the severity of the situation."

"Both myself and the ICU physician have been doing that. The patient and her husband are adamant!"

I waddled into my car and started off on the all too familiar trek to the hospital. I tried to deflect my thoughts from my current situation and towards the fact that in two weeks my life would be totally different. I would be off on maternity leave, two weeks before Logan was due. There would be a few weeks with no intrusion from my past life of nighttime call and my future life of nighttime feedings. I was definitely looking forward to this. I was definitely ready.

I pulled into my space in the parking enclosure and weaved my way through the labyrinth of hallways toward the intensive care unit. I rushed, as much as I could in my present condition, past a series of patient rooms and remembered back to the time when one of my patients had succumbed to melanoma in the prime of her life. It really hit a surgeon hard when a young person was taken too soon. I reflected on whether this was where I was headed again this evening. Sometimes one could feel so impotent in this profession.

I entered through the front doors of the ICU and made my way over to the bed with all the commotion. Robert was speaking with Dr. Rebecca Jennings, the physician working in the ICU that evening. I headed over to them as quickly as my ever-expanding habitus would allow.

"How ... is ... it ... going?" I asked as I panted and turned my gaze toward the head of the bed. I could see that they were getting ready to intubate the patient. I was not going to be able to speak with her. I often found it disconcerting when I had to determine a patient's wishes through friends or family members when I was dealing with something so acute and potentially life threatening.

"Not good," Robert replied. "We are going to need to intubate her. Her present hemoglobin is 66 and we have ongoing blood loss."

"Where is her husband?"

"He is in the family room. Let me introduce you."

Robert and I headed out to the ICU waiting room and into one of the private rooms. There were three men, two women, and unexpectedly, two very young children.

"Mr. Caisson, this is Dr. Jones, my attending surgeon," Robert stated.

"Hello, Mr. Caisson. I am sorry we have to meet under such difficult circumstances."

"Thank you. These are my brothers and sisters and these are my children, Samantha and Charlie."

"Hello!" I exclaimed, turning my attention toward the children. "Is it all right if I speak with your daddy for a moment?"

They both nodded, saying nothing.

Mr. Caisson, Robert and I left the room and closed the door behind us. We started walking back toward the ICU and entered a smaller, private room just outside.

"Mr. Caisson, I am afraid we have a very difficult situation. Your wife appears to be bleeding from her entire stomach. We don't know why and that is not important. It is unlikely we can stop this without an operation to remove most if not all of her stomach. This is difficult to do at the best of times, and it is especially difficult in urgent situations. I think that it will be very difficult to do without blood to support her through this.

"No blood products! You can do whatever you wish, however she and I discussed this. There will be no blood products. She will be refused entrance into heaven if you give her blood."

I fought back the urge to say what I was truly thinking. What would be the benefit of pulling this young woman from her children's lives when they were such a young age?

Robert interjected, "I have spoken with hematology and there is no time for blood substitutes."

"I know," replied Mr. Caisson flatly. "Please take her for surgery and do what you have to do."

I looked directly into his bloodshot and tear-stained eyes. "I want you to know that it is unlikely that we can save her without the use of blood products. It is likely that she will die on the table."

"You do not know that! Please try."

I swiftly explained the operation to him and called the ICU. I reiterated that I was uncomfortable and that she would likely die on the table.

He turned and walked out the door and into the ICU to be with his wife. I decided to leave their last few moments together devoid of my questioning, intrusive thoughts and feelings.

The operating room was preparing, and the anesthesiologist was speaking to Mr. Caisson who seemed to remain emotionless. I suspected that his values were screaming loudly behind his flat demeanor, just as mine were screaming behind mine.

Just as we were about to get ready to roll the bed out to the operating room, the patient's head nurse yelled out. "The blood pressure is $50/25$, and it looks like the patient is going into a life-threatening dysrhythmia. We need to start CPR!"

Everyone jumped into action, while the patient's husband stood at the end of the bed in disbelief. No one asked him to leave as there was recent evidence that family members do better if they are allowed to be present during resuscitative efforts. I was not sure how I felt about this. Given the circumstances, I was sure that this would probably be the last opportunity that he would ever have to see his wife, the mother of his young children, alive, before her important part in their lives would be silenced forever.

"What is going on?" he yelled.

I made my way to the end of the bed and positioned myself next to him. "I am afraid that her body is telling us that without blood products, blood that would support the important functions of her heart, brain and other organs, she will likely pass away. This is very serious. I cannot take her to the operating room in this condition. We will need to try to get her blood pressure up with fluids and stabilize her before I can operate."

"How long will that take?"

"I don't know. I don't know if we will even be effective in keeping her alive long enough to get her to the operating room."

"You can't operate or you won't operate!" He was now yelling at me.

I decided that it would be best to return to the small

room outside the ICU where we could speak without the distraction of impending death intruding into our conversation. I suggested this and guided him aggressively out the doors of the ICU and into a private room.

"Mr. Caisson, I am going to be completely honest with you."

"I wish you would be."

"I have thought about refusing to operate as I think that it would be very difficult for all involved if we are not allowed to use blood products. I feel that there would be very little chance that we could save her."

"You don't know that for sure!" he said in a voice that appeared several octaves lower than the one I had been assaulted with in the intensive care unit.

"If I did not know it then, I most certainly am sure of it now! What is happening now is her body telling us that she is near death if we do not consider the use of blood products to support her." I said this with the intention to support and inform him, not to persuade him in any way. Seeing how defeated he seemed, I leaned forward and put my hand on his shoulder. "This is difficult for myself and my team. I am sure it is many times more difficult for you!"

"Why won't you save her with surgery? Take out her stomach!"

"She continues to bleed. What her body is telling us is that she is almost out of her own blood and that if we do not support her for that she will have a tough time pulling through."

"How long have you been a surgeon? Have you seen this before?"

Oh great, it was going to be like that. It had been a long

The Death of Motherhood

time since I had been accosted with that question, and I had chalked it up to my aging appearance and my more confident nature over time. I had often wondered how often my male colleagues had been asked this very same question and lamented that this was twice in the same number of days that I appeared to have been questioned as a result of my gender. Luckily, I had been questioned enough in the past to allow me to construct an eloquent response.

"I am not as young as I look. I have been a surgeon for well over 10 years and have experience in this area. If we had the time, I would be happy to offer you a second or third opinion. Unfortunately, I do not think we have the luxury of time!"

There was a knock at the door, and I opened it to reveal Robert. The look on his face said it all. I waved him in, and he chose an unoccupied seat which was strategically located right next to Mr. Caisson. I knew that the next thirty seconds would be devastating and life changing.

Robert laid his hand on Mr. Caisson's left shoulder in a sympathetic, but awkward way. This is how it always seemed.

Robert began, "I am sorry, Mr. Caisson, but your wife has passed away."

Mr. Caisson looked back and forth between the two of us in disbelief. It seemed like we were there for an eternity. I moved over to Mr. Caisson's right side and placed my hand on his right shoulder.

"I am so sorry," I murmured. I just stood there, bowing my head and thinking about the depths of despair that were winding their way in to take over the entire room.

Mr. Caisson placed his head in his hands and let out a blood curdling scream. Then, he started to cry—it was low and soft at first and then got steadily louder as it ascended into a full-fledged bawl.

He turned towards me with tears in his eyes. "I am sorry I questioned—" he stammered.

"It's all right. I cannot even begin to imagine what you are going through. Would you like to spend some time with your wife?" I asked.

"Yes," he replied, while looking directly at me. "Thank you,"

"You are welcome."

Robert and I led Mr. Caisson back to bed 14. The nurses had covered up everything except the patient's face. Even the room was tidy. I appreciated that they had been able to take care of these very important details in such short order. The patient's hair was brushed, and she looked peaceful. Mr. Caisson went over to his wife and laid his hand on her head. He leaned over and kissed her and laid his body against hers. I decided that now was the time for me to take my leave. I turned and exited quietly.

As was common in situations like these, I had no idea what the patient's name was. It was strange that I had had a more intimate experience with her than the other members of her immediate family, yet I only knew their names. I went over to her chart to retrieve a sticker with her personal information. As I looked down at the name, I stared in disbelief. I looked up at the enclosed curtains of bed 14 and back down at the nameplate—Logan Rose Caisson. How truly unbelievable! Earlier in the day I had been using the name Logan in communicating with my soon to be firstborn son, and now I was using it as witness to the very difficult death of a young mother.

My thoughts came back to how exhausted I was. It seemed as if it took less and less for me to achieve this state as the days of my pregnancy passed along. I placed my hands over my expanding belly and realized that I had almost completely forgotten about my pregnancy over the last several hours. I thought about how lucky I was. The relationship between myself and Logan had only been temporarily breeched for a few hours. The relationship between Logan Rose and her children, Samantha and Charlie, had been silenced forever.

18
Alone with Logan

It was just two weeks later, one day after I went off on maternity leave, when Logan arrived. I was very excited that he was being born in the fall, my favorite season. I intended to remember every moment of it. Until it happened ...

The contractions began in the middle of a fabulous October morning where the sunlight was warm and the air was cool. I was sitting in my sunroom, and for several hours I breathed my way through it. I was alone, with Silence, and enjoying every moment of it. When the contractions got to be about ten minutes apart, I called my labour coach, Cynthia, who had been a great friend and confidante for me over the last several years. We had been to prenatal classes together with many other 'couples'. Both of us understood that my health care directive was epidural first, baby second. We both knew the order.

The phone conversation between Cynthia and I was the first glimpse I had into the lack of control that was going to step in and take over during what I had envisioned was going to be the very logical and highly controlled birth of my eldest child. I had approached prenatal classes head

Alone with Logan

on with the understanding that my goal was going to be to preserve as much control as possible during the whole process. Otherwise, what was the point?

I was immediately irritated as Cynthia did not pick up on my unyielding intrusion until the fourth ring. I had intentionally waited until a contraction had passed and was prepared to complete our entire telephone conversation before the next contraction set in.

"Hello?" she answered in what I thought was a somewhat noncommittal tone.

"Hello, it's Tori! I have been having contractions for the last several hours and they are now about ten minutes apart. I think it is time to get to the hospital."

"Great, I am just going to wait five minutes until the contractors who are painting my house clean up and leave and then I will be right over. This is going to be so exciting!"

"Five minutes? This is not how we practiced it. We agreed that I would call and you would be right over. Is that not what we agreed to?" I could hear the rise in the tone of my voice in parallel with the next contraction coming on. I just needed to get Cynthia off the line.

"Yes, I'll be right over! The contractors are just leaving now, and I am not even allowing the door to close behind them."

Cynthia arrived on my doorstep ten minutes later, just as we had rehearsed. I was always very much in favour of planning everything, and I was not going to be deterred by the slight transgression that our telephone call had exacted on an otherwise perfectly developed plan. I smiled to myself.

"Hello, Cynthia. Are you ready for this?"

"Are you ready for this? For all of this?"

"Definitely! Onward and upward as they say."

We made small talk in discrete seven to eight-minute intervals, punctuated by my ill-controlled breathing and strings of high-pitched obscenities. As we made our way toward the hospital, my hospital, I reflected on the events that had unraveled several weeks earlier when I had observed another mother succumb to her untimely demise. During the most intense peaks of each contraction, I begged to be taken and to join this less fortunate mother in what I perceived to be a far more relaxed and comfortable place. The only thing that kept me going was the recognition that this was the day when Logan and I would formally meet each other face to face for the very first time. That, and the promise of an epidural.

Cynthia dropped me off at the front door and went to park the car. Within a few minutes, we were directed into a very posh room on the Labour and Delivery floor. It was much more lavish than nearly any bedroom I had ever been in before. I threw my Burberry overnight bag on the bed and started to change into the standard issue uniform for this institution. How funny it was to be on the other side!

The contractions were stronger now, almost unbearable, and I was wondering if there were any obscenities I had failed to take advantage of.

Dr. Barkley entered the room. "Good afternoon, Tori! We are finally here!"

I tried my best to remain civil while she examined me. Aside from a few renditions of 'get me my fucking epidural', I thought I had done remarkably well. A look of surprise came over her face.

"What is going on?" I panted.

"I am afraid you are too far along for an epidural. You are nine centimetres dilated and almost ready to push. You have done a very good job in making your way through this!"

"Fuck!" I screamed in disbelief. "What the hell does this mean?"

"You have done a very good job thus far," Dr. Barkley explained in a very calm and clear voice. I imagined that she was used to this type of aggressive, unfocused questioning. "We can give you something through the IV and we can coach you along. I am sure you will do great!"

What more was there to say? "Fuck, OK," I acquiesced.

Thirty minutes later, with Cynthia on one side and Dr. Barkley coaching me through the pushing process, I was wondering how I ever got myself into this fucking situation. A lack of planning was not my suit and the degree of loss of control I felt was definitely disheartening.

"I am not doing this!" I exclaimed after each contraction. "What a fucking conspiracy the two of you have put together against me! Leave me the fuck alone."

The room went from the three of us and 'you are doing fine' after each contraction to a more and more crowded mainstream event with little noise other than my cursive screams. If it weren't for me, the room would have no noise at all. I looked up and thought, *at what point did this supposed miraculous event evolve into such an exciting, standing room only performance?*

Dr. Barkley stood up and looked me directly in the eyes. "We need to do an emergency Caesarean!" she exclaimed.

"The baby is not doing well, and you are getting tired. We need to get the baby out!"

"Logan, you need to get Logan out! That is what you mean. He has a name you know. His name is Logan!" I screamed. "Do what you have to do."

I was wheeled into the operating room and told to count backward from one hundred. That, as they say, is all I remember. I had plans, I was going to be there for all of it. That, however, was all she wrote.

The first thing I remember was waking up with Cynthia asking me how I was. She said that Logan was just great and that he was the longest baby that they had ever seen. She commented that Dr. Barkley had said that she was not surprised that I had to be rushed in for an emergency C-section. Perhaps she could have told me that before the whole contraction and pushing bullshit. Jesus, that was not even my idea. I had to be talked into that! We had argued about it. I would say things like 'I don't do the labour thing' and she had retorted, 'You should try it as it is the safest'. I should have listened to my intuition.

I brought myself back to reality. "When can I see Logan?" I asked.

"They are bringing him over right now! He is so beautiful. He definitely takes after his mother!"

The door opened to a small Asian woman who seemed to be dressed almost entirely in baby blue. "Baby Logan!" she exclaimed, almost with motherly pride.

She brought Logan over and placed him in my arms. I looked down at this figuratively small being and directly into the same piercing blue eyes that I saw with my own reflection. His perfectly round head had a small tuft of black hair perched directly on top.

"He definitely has his mother's good looks!" I exclaimed as I turned toward Cynthia and smiled.

The next few hours seemed almost surreal as people came and went. There were people checking on me, people checking on Logan and people checking on the two of us together. We were introduced, as a couple, to our first joint effort—breastfeeding. It seemed that he was more into it than I was. Perhaps because his survival depended on it. I smiled at my perverse logic.

At about 2:00 a.m., Cynthia got up to leave. I thanked her for everything and for sticking around for so long. She stated that she would be back later that morning and that she would bring my parents with her. They had, unfortunately, not been planning that Logan would arrive early. Their flight had landed at about the same time Logan arrived! We had spoken on the phone, of course, but formal introductions would have to wait until later today.

Cynthia got up to leave. Just before she closed the door behind her, she said, "I guess you and your old friend Silence will have to put your relationship on the back burner for a while, a long while!"

I smiled and thought about how well she knew me. With that she was gone, leaving Logan and I to fend for ourselves for the very first time.

19
When Silence is Complete

Logan and I had managed to create a number of fabulous memories, both before and after the planned arrival of Lucas. At fourteen, Logan was starting to see himself more as an adult, rather than teetering back and forth between being a boy and being a man, and I was recognizing the importance of the stories I had to tell. I knew that he was concerned about what 'truths' would come out in the so called 'fictional' re-enactment of our lives to date. I could not personally recall the waves of embarrassment that I must have felt as a teenager when a part of me was about to be revealed to the world, and thus I could only imagine the extent of his concern. I had assured him that he had nothing to worry about, however I was grappling with how much the words and events needed to be continually massaged in order that they could truly be considered fiction. I had been told that introductory works of fiction by new authors tended to be more truth than not.

I had taken several months to develop the first seven chapters of the novel. I toyed with the development of the characters, especially those that were very central to the importance of the main theme—the Silence of

Motherhood. I again pondered how many different ways the story of silence could be told; how many examples I had either experienced personally or knew of through others. There had been stories of tragic events unraveling despite motherhood and in parallel with motherhood, stories where the suffering of motherhood existed unbeknownst to the outside world, and even stories of the loss of either one arm or the other of the mother-child relationship.

I sat down to try and bring Chapter Eight to life. My motivation on this lovely fall day was nothing more than the fact that the weather demanded it. I always felt a sense of renewal and hope when the mornings presented themselves with just that touch of a reminder that summer would not last forever. This was the season that pulled colour into the leaves and inspired me toward action. I knew that over the next several months I was likely to be successful at whatever I set out to do.

I wanted Chapter Eight to tell one of the most personal stories of how motherhood had been silenced in my life. There were many examples, but none more raw than the loss of the child from the mother-child equation. My experience, I was sure, had been a chapter in the lives of thousands, if not millions, of women dating back to the start of the human experience, if not before. I was sure that my experience was not the easiest, nor the hardest, chapter ever written. It was, however, the only one that I was left alone to experience from start to finish. I often wondered about attaching the word finish to this experience. I don't believe that the loss of a child, whenever the woman chooses to define the start of the life for her child, is ever truly finished. Perhaps it was best described as from start to eternity.

I sat down and knew that this was The Chapter that would be the namesake of the book, and thus I wrote 'Chapter 8 – The Silence of Motherhood'.

20
Motherhood Silenced

I was going to write about the loss of my pregnancy following the first cycle of donor insemination. I knew there would be a lot of emotion tied to this, emotion that would underlie any fiction that I would add to the recipe of this part of my life story. I began...

> *The chorionic villus sampling was scheduled for two weeks in the future. Although I was no stranger to misfortune, having suffered the loss of a significant relationship and a close family member during my surgical residency, the wait for confirmation of my known fate was almost unbearable.*

I was concerned about how The Chapter might unfold, but the words seemed to be flowing easily from my heart, through my fingers, into the keyboard and onto the screen in front of me. I wondered how many women had experienced what I was about to put into writing for the first time. This was a thought that haunted me often. The whole world seemed to go on as if nothing had ever happened; nothing had ever happened to me and nothing had ever happened to any of these other women. These women walked through the world, most of them in silence, while the events of the day, some of them bearing on their future reproductive health, were being decided almost in parallel with their unfortunate fate. It was foreign to me how discussions about women's reproductive decisions seemed to surface and resurface, time and again. There had been a lot in the literature lately about restriction of sperm donation to couples—heterosexual couples! There were many who would be negatively impacted if this became a reality, myself included. It was like a race against time to get in under the wire and be one of the lucky ones. I knew, logically, that changes like this moved at a snail's pace. However, that did little to quell the emotion tied to ensuring that my life, with a child, would remain within the realm of possibility.

Adding to the anxiety with respect to The Chapter was the emotionality itself. Not being known as someone with intense outward expression of emotion, I tended to wear my emotions close to my chest. At times there seemed to be such a discordance between the strength of the feelings lying just below the surface and the outward appearance of a stony resilience. It was not that the surface was never pulled back to reveal this raw compendium of my inner soul—many had first-hand knowledge of this transformative Dr. Jones to Ms. Hyde event. However, this 'fictional' account meant that others would be able to open a previously unopened vault and have ready access to parts of my inner life that were infrequently displayed, even to myself.

I thought about how I imagined all women dealt with this type of loss, especially those like myself without any religious predilection. How many times had I told myself that 'this was fate' or 'this was how it was meant to be'? All the while I was asking myself if this was a logical way to think about the course of events. There was a fine line between the belief in fate and the belief in a superior being, even though I could make up all kinds of excuses as to how my concept of reality was based in a solid scientific truth. If this part of the story had not happened, then Logan would not exist—obviously it was fate! I was sure that every woman who had survived this, as I had so painfully done, felt this way about their future children—that they would not exist were it not for the horrible pain associated with the dissolution of a previous mother-child relationship. This was my fate; Logan and eventually Lucas were my fate.

I picked up my glass of New Zealand Sauvignon Blanc and took a long, satisfying sip. Logan was out with friends at the community centre and Lucas was at a friend's house for what seemed like just another in a long line of sleepovers. Again, I had the house to myself. Silence was becoming less painful and more like the old friend I used to know. I was getting more comfortable with the new relationship that was developing between us. Like an old married couple, Silence and I were learning the next steps in the dance that was unfolding between us. Telling my story and the story of the other women and their relationship with the invisibility of motherhood was gratifying and extremely motivating. It was much different than the masculine world that I lived in from sunup to sunup almost every day. It was refreshing, even when the stories delved into the deepest and darkest parts of a fractured relationship. I continued with my composition ...

At every interaction, I thought about how many others around me were holding potentially devastating secrets, close to their hearts, that no one else knew about. I methodically carried out my normal activities—evaluating patients, performing surgeries, comforting patients and family members. I found myself wondering, many times per day, how ironic it was that I was the one closest to the brink. Who was there to save me? Who was there to comfort me?

I closed my eyes, leaned back, and envisioned the excruciating emotion and lack of emotion that lay behind the construction of this paragraph. These few hours seemed like a lifetime, and even now I could retrace every thought and every feeling to the second that it had happened. I remembered how surreal every movement seemed; how I initially made it through each and every minute by counting the number of breaths that I would take until I became completely numb and would no longer have to dwell on what was happening. And just like that, it would come searing back into my consciousness. I interacted with patients, performed mechanistically in the operating theatre and attended required administrative duties like I was not even there. I wondered how long it would last before I would begin to feel some relief—days, weeks, months, years, perhaps longer? In a fast-paced world, we had come to expect that the resolution of everything would be swift. Then, we faced a situation where we had to deal with our own emotions; emotions that we had felt before, but never with such intensity. We had to deal with them, expected quick resolution, and were surprised when we awoke day after day to the same intense numb, searing feeling.

Then one day, there is a slightly different and lighter feeling. It doesn't start acutely, rather it builds from a slow hum, almost imperceptible to the human mind, and especially the human heart. It doesn't last. It fades almost as quickly as it first arrived, but it does not hide forever. It returns, slightly louder and slightly longer the next time. It interrupts the long periods of pain and returns one to the normal perception of everyday life. You realize that you are actually present when patients are speaking to you and that you are actually the one performing surgeries and saving lives.

I glanced up at the screen in front of me. How strange that there are certain events in our lives that we relive almost as if they are unraveling for the very first time. As my mind wandered through the next few paragraphs, I could almost hear the halls of the hospital, see the myriad of patients and others that crossed my path, feel the touch of the patients' hands as I soothed them off to sleep, and smell the calm smooth air of summer. It was as if it was happening for the very first time. The emotions were always the same, always intense and unrelenting.

It was somewhat satisfying that the words were flowing so smoothly. The emotion seemed to be more of a strength than the impediment I feared that it would be. This was, after all, where the story truly began for me. It was the place that I would keep coming back to. It was intense, yet surreal and numbing.

I took another sip of wine and noted that my glass was

almost empty. I had not been aware of how intensely my being had been wrapped up in telling this small part of the story. Several hours had passed, and there were a string unanswered texts from Logan asking how and where I was.

5:20 p.m.—Hi, Mom! How ya doing?
5:40 p.m.—Hi, Mom?
6:17 p.m.—Where r u? At community centre. Going to a movie.
6:49 p.m.—Buying movie tickets. Going to Arrival.

I glanced at the time—7:05 p.m. I texted that I had been writing and that I was okay. Almost instantly the screen flashed ...

7:06 p.m.—Good! Was worried. Signing off for movie.

I turned my attention back to my laptop screen with the realization that the unyielding, relived emotion had now almost completely dissipated. I refrained from reviewing what had just been written as I knew that it was the most perfect and most accurate account of what had happened. I was exhausted and did not want to re-invoke the intensity of emotion that I had just experienced. I understood that there would be countless visits back, but not tonight. The Chapter seemed to be begging for a short concluding statement, which would open the door to an exploration of all the ways in which motherhood could be overlooked...

> ***With that, I hung up and thought about how easily motherhood could be silenced. Little did I know that I had only just begun to scratch the surface.***

21
My One-Year Goals

Those first few months with just Logan and myself were a blur, as I am sure they are for most first-time parents. There is no way to warn someone about the full onslaught of motherhood. You will never exist again in this universe without being connected to this small being. It was no different for me.

I always told myself that motherhood would be bearable as long as it was not as difficult as a surgical residency, and it never was. I never allowed the nights to be interrupted by light or movement. Nighttime requests for attention were met with only a soothing hug, a gentle hum and the offering of the left or right boob depending on where we were in the feeding cycle. Logan lay next to me under the veil of complete silence and darkness. The only movement was me shifting from one side of the king-sized bed to the other by deftly navigating myself over Logan as he awoke, so that he was never offered the same boob twice in a row. I thought that it worked magnificently!

I had no preconceived ideas about breastfeeding. If it worked, it worked, and if it didn't, oh well! Like most women, I found it convenient. Not the type of convenience that one finds in being close to a grocery store on the way home from work. It was more like the type of convenience that allows one to survive another day in an otherwise chaotic world. It allows one to preserve a few minutes to get to the washroom when they need to, eat a stale cracker for lunch, or brush one's teeth—activities that the rest of the world takes for granted. I referred to these activities as my After-Logan list.

When I compared the After-Logan (AL) list to the Before-Logan (BL) list, I became acutely aware of how I normally had processed my life, on an everyday basis, before I had a child. I was very much someone who was goal oriented and phenomenally focused on my future. I had my life charted out for the next year, three years, five years, etc. I had never been acutely jettisoned into a situation where I felt like I was either going to scream or where I was fighting for my survival. During those first few weeks, I thought about how I was to meld the person I was, or rather the person I had been, with the person that I was now supposed to be—whomever that was. The only way that I felt I could do this was by sticking to a list of goals. Not a list that held the same great potential of my current one-, three-, and five-year goals, but a list that would allow me to endure and survive one day at a time.

When this idea originally surfaced into my reality, I sat for several minutes (remember I was trying to merely survive and could not afford any longer) reflecting on my one-year goals. I noted that they were very tidy and compact goals, which seemed to almost reach out and pull me into the screen. They were screaming at me 'This is who you are! Remember to follow us!' Although we had only known each other for a very short time, we felt comfortable with each other and we were both headed in the same direction. I could almost see the conversation developing in my head.

"Follow us," my one-year goals urged. "You know that we represent your destiny."

"Not now! Can't you see by looking at me that I am too tired? I am working so hard just to keep my head above water. Surely you remember me speaking to you about the arrival of Logan? Logan, my son, is now here. There is no room for us to continue to walk hand in hand into the future at this time. I need you to understand that I must bid you adieu, for now, and we may even need to re-evaluate our friendship at some point in the future."

My one-year goals seemed perplexed. "We don't understand. We have known each other for only a very short period of time, and we vaguely remember the mention of Logan from our last encounter. However, we have always brought out the best in you! You told us on more than one occasion that we were where you were most comfortable and where you wanted to go. Your three- and five-year goals also have an investment in this. Are you 'shelving all of us' as it were?"

"I don't know." It seemed as if it were all I could do to get my butt out of the chair from time to time, and I was now being asked to run a marathon. And I don't even like running!

"What do you mean you don't know? That is not the type of answer that I would expect from Dr. Victoria Jones!"

I knew that I should reflect on this for a moment, as one commonly does when they are contemplating a change in the status of a relationship with someone important. I was also expecting my one-year goals to help me define the future relationship with my three- and five-year goals. I was not looking forward to facing them all at the same time.

I started slowly. "I am not, nor will I ever be, the same person that I was when we first met. Logan has changed who I am, and that will be reflected in all my relationships, most certainly the ones that I have with you and my three- and five-year goals. I trust that our relationship will still continue to exist, although altered, in ways that I can't even begin to imagine! I need to add another to our enclave; one that is more urgent and aimed at one-week or even one-day goals. I hope that you can understand that this relationship, with the new member of the team, will take precedence for now. You need to allow me some room to evaluate where you and I are headed in the future."

"I am not sure we understand," my one-year goals retorted. "Get back to us when you figure out what you need from us, if anything." And with that, my one-year goals moved to a position that was foreign to both of us—not recognizing if we would ever recover our relationship in the future. Only time and some degree of persistence would tell.

I decided that my relationship with my immediate goals would be more basic. Both of us needed to be constantly aware of each other's presence if this was going to work. These were to be rudimentary goals, goals that would see both Logan and I survive those early months, or possibly even longer. I had no idea how to gauge where this was going. Flexible goals were not a concept that I was used to or that I was particularly enamoured with.

I thought about those things that needed to get accomplished in order that I might survive for twenty-four hours, one day at a time. I knew that this had to be centred around me in order for Logan to survive as well. Just like medicine, if the mother survived, then the baby survived. I thought about having five things on the list—not too long, but long enough that I would feel a sense of accomplishment that would fuel me on toward the next twenty-four hours. At first, I thought about how silly this sounded, and then I brought myself back into the realm of my absolute need to have some framework for how we were going to survive. The two words were becoming synonymous—survival and success.

Fueled mostly by desperation, a glass of orange juice and a few handfuls of almonds—all that was readily available and would most certainly be considered a meal—I started to compose the first version of the list. It was not called the After-Logan list, rather it was just entitled 'The 24-hour list for survival of Victoria and Logan'. I thought it was simple and that it outlined exactly what the purpose of the mission was. The list read as follows:

1. Get up
2. Brush teeth
3. Eat a meal
4. Drink water
5. Sleep

There was no defined order to the list, and I was impressed that it represented everything I probably needed to achieve, for myself, to make it from one day to the next, even one hour to the next. I was satisfied with how simple life could be if one just brought it down to the basics. I could be successful without even leaving the comfort of my own home, given the prevalence of delivery options at my disposal.

As expected, my one-, three- and five-year goals were not as impressed with me as I was with myself. They arose from the dark reaches of my grey matter to remind me that these were small, almost insignificant goals, and that they were certainly goals that were below what they had come to expect from me. They were concerned for themselves in that they were all related to each other, in some way, and seemed to flow from one to the next. I always considered them as a group, and moved back and forth easily between each member, making adjustments as time and circumstances allowed. We met at least once a month, and everyone was always excited about the opportunity for growth after my annual performance review with my Chair, Dr. Christias. Not only were these new goals out of line with this type of process, they were now going to supersede everyone else in the group! My compadre of goals had not even been aware that this type of recruitment was going to be necessary—no one had consulted them!

I tried to explain that this was an unforeseen circumstance and that immediate action was necessary. I was not dissolving my relationships with them, rather I was incorporating a new member, which could make us all stronger. This was as foreign and uncomfortable for me as it was for them, and I hoped that once we were back to a more normal state of affairs this would no longer be necessary.

I reflected on the absurdity of the fact that I represented all members of the group separately and simultaneously. I was at once in conversation with my present, former and future selves. I/we recognized that things would never be the same between us again and I/we were all uncomfortable as I/we had always been very regimented in our

My One-Year Goals

approach to planning for our future. This new element was the simplest and the most important, yet the least well understood by all of us. I/we agreed to re-explore the relationships in one month's time to see if things were working.

I/we were to rest assured that this was only for a very short time. I/we would return, in short order, to something that more accurately reflected our previous state.

As I got up to get a pen to cross 'Eat a meal' off the 24-hour list, I reflected on which item I would work toward next. I was comforted by the brilliance of this short-term solution and that I/we had been able to agree upon this as a group. It was then that I heard a new and unfamiliar voice arise from the most accessible parts of my mind.

"Thank you for inviting me to be a part of your community," my 24-hour list said. "I look forward to a long and enduring relationship with each of you."

"Oh, shit!" I thought in unison with the remaining members of the group. This new element seemed confident that they were going to be with us for longer than any of us could have expected or imagined.

22
Nanny Chronicles I

It was approximately six weeks later, and Logan, the 24-hour list and I had fallen into full stride. My one-, three- and five-year goals had not been heard from in several weeks. It seems that they had been reassured by the fact that I had promised to arrange for my annual performance review with Dr. Christias sometime within the next six months. I had never realized how unidimensional my relationships with them had been. Although I/we all seemed to care about each other, it was all based on forward movement and academic success. This new relationship with the 24-hour list was taking some getting used to, and I seemed to be the only one willing to try. I think the rest of the group felt that the 24-hour list would hopefully just disappear from the group as quickly as it had arrived. At least that was the feeling that I was left with after our scheduled one month follow up meeting. I set all of this to the back of my mind.

I needed to start to think about expanding my scope beyond my new best friend, the 24-hour list, but not to the extent that I was ready to invite my old friends back into the fold. I needed to find a nanny, the person who would care for Logan as I prepared to return to my professional life. I had started to do some work on this before Logan arrived, however I was now ready to move full speed ahead. I was confident that I was going to be successful in finding someone who was going to fit right in. After all, I kept telling myself, nothing would ever be as hard as a surgical residency. All that was about to change. Finding a nanny was going to prove to be almost the hardest thing that I had ever done.

I sat down with the director from the agency that I had chosen to work with. It was a well-respected and reputable agency that had managed to find certified nannies for a lot of my friends. I had been unaware of how long it would take to find someone; however, the agency was hopeful that they could work with me.

It was a Saturday morning, and I was feeling confident as I had already crossed get up, eat a meal, brush teeth and drink water off of my 24-hour list. In fact, I was starting to think about updating the 24-hour list. I was becoming quite successful at crossing off everything, every day, repeatedly, day after day. The brushing teeth item was the hardest to achieve, however I had not missed that for almost twelve straight days in a row! Further, I was accomplishing more and more every day! When I first became acquainted with my 24-hour list, there were many days when I had stood in front of a mirror and was thankful that I had not included 'take a shower', 'put on deodorant', or 'brush hair' on the list. Now I was accomplishing each and every one of these tasks on a daily basis!

This was the day that the director, Karen, and I were going to sit down and interview seven candidates for the position of Dr. Victoria Jones' nanny. Logan and I had slept well the night before, and as I said previously, I was extremely confident.

It started off somewhat slowly. The first two candidates were unable to accept the extent of responsibility that went along with the job, even after I described what was necessary. One was pursuing a teaching certificate at the local college and one seemed more obsessed with telling me how she was going to use her weekends to return to her family some two hours away. I explained to each of them how their vision for how this was going to unfold was not congruent with what was needed. I thanked each of them for taking the time to interview.

"Karen, these are not the kind of people that I am looking for! There needs to be more of an understanding that I am a single parent with a very demanding job. I need someone who is going to be willing to live-in and who will be dedicated to raising Logan with me."

"Relax!" she exclaimed, placing her hand on my knee as I finished feeding Logan. "I just wanted to start with a few examples of what is commonly out there. More than eighty per cent of our clients come from families where there are two parents, so that has tended to be our target audience. A truly single parent family, not just divorced couples where both parents are actively involved to a greater or lesser degree, is relatively new to us. It is a challenge that our company is willing to rise to and where we think we can be truly innovative and successful."

"I hope so! I think that you will find that women in my situation are going to become an increasingly common part of your clientele. I know several other women who are pursuing this, and the statistics show that it is an increasingly common way for women to recognize their dream of having it all."

"I recognize that. We are aware of the statistics, and we are increasingly working with similar organizations to explore different ways of identifying the appropriate individuals. I think that the next two candidates will be more to your liking. They are certainly more open to exploring being a larger part of your family than most of the nannies we have traditionally worked with. They both come highly recommended from another agency that has worked with both of them previously. They each have had one previous employer where their services were no longer deemed necessary. Both were amicable departures."

"OK," I sighed. "Let's see where this will take us."

She opened the door to a young, slight woman, whom I thought could not be more than eighteen years of age. She was comfortably dressed in a loose purple hoodie, jeans and well-worn sneakers. I noted that her light brown hair was shoulder length and neatly brushed and that her nails were short and unpolished. Probably both characteristics of a good nanny. I am not sure what evidence I was using to support this, but it sounded good to me. I felt that I was trying to convince myself of the positives given the current situation.

"Hello," she said, extending her hand toward me. "I'm Lorraine."

"Hi, Lorraine," I replied as I shook her hand. As I leaned toward her, she unobtrusively slipped Logan out of my arms and into her own. Logan did not flinch. He did not even seem to notice, to be honest. She began to interview me about what was required for the job. She wanted to ensure that she was going to be allowed to do what was best for Logan and that we would be able to work together to care for him. It seemed as if she was paying her undivided attention to our conversation and also to Logan. She wandered towards the fridge, opened the door, and asked whether she would be feeding Logan formula or breast milk. She glanced over at me, and almost instinctively added, "I don't care which—want to be prepared."

She closed the door and walked back towards me. "He seems very contented. How is the sleeping going?"

"All right. He wakes up to eat and that is about all. I try not to disturb him during those times. I try not to even move him."

"Great! When you are away I will just hold a bottle by him?"

"Yes, that would be best for all." I responded as if I were the resident expert on the care of small, helpless creatures.

We continued on, discussing various aspects of childcare, hours of work and other chit-chat for about fifteen minutes. It appeared that we were aligned on almost all aspects of the care of Logan, and that this was potentially going to be a great match.

"When would you be able to start?" I asked.

"Within the week."

The three of us discussed logistics. She would be a live-in nanny, have somewhat regular hours, but be available for whatever was needed. I would be present for the first three weeks, and then we would need to speak several times per day to ensure things were going according to my plan. My first full night on call would be in three months, and I was hoping that we would all be comfortable with the situation by that time. We agreed that she would start the following Monday.

The first week flew by without a hitch. Lorraine and I were getting to know each other better, and Logan was settling in. Lorraine stayed in her room in the basement, for the most part, during the evening hours. It was as if Logan and I had the house to ourselves, and it was wonderful. We were falling into a rhythm—I knew what to expect from both of them, Logan knew what to expect from both of us, and Lorraine knew what to expect from the family Jones. By the third week, there would be no stopping us. We were a well-oiled machine, and I was at the helm. Why I thought it would or should remain this way, I will never know.

I returned to full time work on a Monday morning. I had been in and out of the office doing paperwork during my 'time off', and thus there was not actually a lot to be done on that first day. I had scheduled a light clinic in the afternoon just to ease back into being a surgeon—not that I was ever anything but a surgeon! People acknowledged my return and welcomed me back, most with a high degree of enthusiasm. All seemed to be going smoothly. I marveled that it was great that I was returning to the helm of my professional life as well. I was certain I would defy all odds and be able to have it all!

I left the hospital at 5:30 p.m. and made my way home. It seemed so funny to think that it would no longer be the same silent return home from work that I was used to. The house would be different now, in a pleasant way I thought. I reflected on the last three weeks and how everyone had been settling into a routine, which would be necessary to sustain this well-oiled machine.

I parked on the street at the front of my house and decided to just allow myself two minutes of complete silence before confronting whatever might lie ahead. I had an ear for Silence, and the two of us just sat there together and enjoyed each other's company for that brief period of time.

I opened the door and stepped out into the cool winter air. I counted the number of steps, as I had done many times in the past, from my car to the front door of my house. There were twenty-seven in total. I discovered the door was locked, as I expected, and thus I withdrew my key. I put it in the keyhole and turned it with a brief click. I opened the door to the warm air that lay within.

At first, I wondered if I was in the right place. The furniture looked familiar, but at the same time it seemed out of place. A large couch lay along the wall where previously an armchair and console had resided. I had to turn the corner into the centre of the room before I could locate all my furniture.

Just then, Lorraine came around the corner with Logan.

"Hello! Do you like what I have done with the place? I thought it would make the room look much more inviting and larger, and I do believe I was right. I don't know what got into me; I just started moving things around and everything just seemed to long for a new and more exciting place!"

I didn't quite know how to reply. I was a creature of

habit and had already imagined myself lounging in a certain way, in a certain place, after my first full day back at work. I gestured with my arm and with my eyes and head as if I were continuing to look around the room and take it all in. It was at that instant that I realized that how I reacted was going to set the tone for the entire future of this new, fragile three-way relationship that we had entered into. I was either going to assert my authority over all things related to my personal life, much like I was used to doing in my professional life, or I was going to let go. I was not very good at the latter.

I brought my attention back to the three of us in the room. I locked eyes with Lorraine who seemed to be eagerly awaiting my reply. With all the skill I could muster, I chose my response wisely. I was not really sure whose needs it was meeting, but I smiled widely and said, "It looks absolutely fabulous! Definitely more open and more functional." This, I knew, was not a lie, but it was a very big step for me. Although it was certainly not the last time where we would be in a similar situation, it was the tone that I wanted to set with Lorraine. I needed her to know that I trusted her with all things, big or small, relating to the well-being of Logan. The smile on her face led me to believe that I had been successful.

23

Single Mother by Choice; Surgeon by Chance?

Logan was approaching his second birthday the summer that we participated, as a couple, in our first Single Mothers by Choice vacation. It was held at a rustic family-based resort in central New England. There was a group of about fifteen women and twenty-two children; the children ranging in age from almost two to almost fourteen. Ten boys and twelve girls in total were ready for a week of fun-filled camp activities. Most of the women had one child, but there were a handful with two, and even one with three! It had never occurred to me, until that very moment when we all first met, that someone might consider walking this treacherous and questionable journey; a journey that was like a lifetime lived from day to day and sometimes hour to hour, more than once. I decided that we were there to enjoy ourselves, not to think about how we might add another to what had become our stable family unit.

Lorraine, Logan and I had fallen into a very comfortable routine over the last almost year and a half. Logan seemed happy and was comfortable when either one of us was around. He was running all over the place and talking up a storm. I knew that we were up for good every morning when he turned his head toward the blackout blinds, and seeing just a wisp of sunlight sneaking in, muttered 'dark gone away!' He knew we were flying out of the 'planeport' to visit a number of families who were similar to ours. I thought it would be a good diversion for a week. When we returned, I was going to have to start looking for a new nanny. Lorraine had given her notice as a full time live-in nanny, and I was still in need of such—nothing less.

The cabin where we were staying was comprised of a single central family area on the second floor leading up, down and over to a series of simple, but comfortable, bedrooms. I was surprised that they were able to accommodate all of us within a single, large living space. I suspected that I should have been just as astonished when a group of a similar size had met several years ago in Colorado when I was just thinking of becoming a mother. Until I had Logan, however, the true reality of the logistics of certain things like this never really truly hit home.

I was assigned to a small room with a twin bed and a very comfortable little cot on the second floor. I noticed that someone had taken the time to place a little stuffed elephant on the cot with a small card beside it which read, 'Welcome home, Logan. Nice to meet you!' I thought it was probably Virginia, the main organizer of the vacation.

The first night at supper I was awestruck by how naturally each family unit of either two, three or four members functioned. We had decided to reserve a large table at the on-site family-based restaurant in order that mothers and children could begin to get to know each other. The restaurant gave us our own room in the back and the children were pretty much allowed the run of the place. I smiled at Logan who was sitting in his booster seat and taking it all in. He tended to be a very reserved young man until he had taken the opportunity to get used to everything and everyone.

I had reunited with Cindy and Hannah from our previous meeting in Colorado some years earlier. Hannah was now ten and had grown significantly, in size and substance, since our last meeting. Her blonde hair was longer now, down to her mid-back, and she wore a pink long-sleeved shirt and dark blue jeans. Her shirt proclaimed 'Cats make the world go around' with the picture of a large tabby cat beneath. I assumed it was a picture of her own cat that had been ironed on. She did not remember me specifically, although she did seem to have fond memories of the large group of women and children she had met sometime in the past. Also present was Teresa. She had also been thinking about motherhood the last time we had met in Colorado. She was now accompanied by a very active four-year-old boy named Tanner. She confided in me that she had been three months pregnant when we first met in Colorado. She had not told anyone as, like most of us, she felt that some things are better left unsaid until they are a certainty.

That first night at dinner we spoke of many things—kids and work and fears and failures, etc. I noted how easy it was to be a part of all of this. I thought back to several years ago and the feeling I had then, as I did now, about how I had found my tribe. I wondered whether it would hold the same fascination if we had lived our normal, average lives, together as a group, day in and day out, rather than seeing each other only for this concentrated period of time once every several years. Like many things in life, something to ponder, but something that would never likely have a real answer.

Virginia, a somewhat overweight and vivacious blonde woman sitting near the head of the table, grabbed her water glass and tapped it with her fork in preparation for discussion of the schedule that was to be placed around the week's activities. It was not foreign to any of us that without some type of structure there would be devolution into chaos that would last not only the length of the week, but which would flow over and into the ensuing month's activities. Once children, and adults for that matter, had a taste of the privilege of a random life, most of them never wanted to go back. That did not mean that there would not be time for celebrations, partying and a good cocktail. However, all of that needed to be placed against a strong foundation of preparation.

"I would like to begin by proposing a toast to a fabulous group of women who are raising a great bunch of kids!" Virginia exclaimed. The clinking of glasses and 'hear, hears!' arose in almost a deafening roar from around the table. "I have been thinking of ways that we can work within a basic schedule, especially for the children, and still have everyone feel like they have had a fantastic vacation." There was unanimous agreement.

"I would like to suggest, with the final count being fifteen mothers and twenty-two children, ten boys and twelve girls, that we divide ourselves into five groups of three parents each. Each mother would be responsible for getting her own children up and ensuring they are ready and have had breakfast. If people know each other or want to team up to do this part that is fine." Victoria looked around, and sensing no early dissention, she continued, "Each group of three women would be responsible for sticking around the complex for one of each of the first five days. People could feel free to come and go as they pleased and partake in all the activities that the resort has to offer. If there is a need for children to stay behind, for instance if they are sick or if they just need a break, then the designated trio of the day could assume care. This would be provided that the child or children and their respective mother were comfortable with this arrangement. I understand this might be easier for the older children, and I understand that some children may not want to part from their mother, however at least it would provide some comfort that there would always be someone 'at home' if needed." The last two days will be a 'free for all' with each parent responsible for their own child or children. I would like to suggest that we all make an attempt, just like tonight, to meet for dinner those last two days. I would like some broader discussion on how the trip worked and what we might do next time, including other potential locations.

Small groups broke out in discussion around the table. People seemed comfortable with the general concept, I think this was because each of us was used to the concept of raising children as being a group project with tentacles reaching far beyond the nuclear family. We decided that the trio of the day would be responsible for providing a breakfast and a dinner choice for the children, and that each mother would agree to check in within one half hour of leaving their child with the trio to ensure that there were no concerns. Checking in could be as simple as an e-mail. We chose our own groups, and it seemed a natural fit that I would be grouped with Cindy and Teresa. They agreed.

"I would also like us to get to know each other as a bigger group, rather than breaking out into smaller cliques or just hanging out with the members from our respective trios." We all agreed that this this was certainly a potential danger. "I would like to suggest that tonight we meet in the large family area, around 9:00 p.m. after most of the children are asleep, to get to know each other better." There was general consensus that this would be a good idea.

The sign-up sheet was being passed around the table. We had arrived on a Friday night and Cindy, Teresa and I assigned ourselves to Day 4, Tuesday. This worked well for our trio as Cindy and Hannah had activities planned for most days except Tuesday. Teresa and I had much the same idea of seeing how the kids behaved in camp on a day-to-day basis, both of us being quite flexible in terms of our schedules.

After supper, Logan and I slowly meandered over to a large sandbox that was in the central courtyard near our complex. It was elevated off the ground by about thirty centimetres. There was one other small boy and his parents who were engrossed in the construction of a colossal sand city. Logan and I chose from amongst a small collection of available plastic, sand-stained toys, mostly vehicles, a few classic pieces, including a cement mixer, dump truck, and a fire engine. We constructed cursory roads within the available space, and with loud exclamations of 'vroom-vroom', proceeded to destroy the roads as seamlessly as they had been built. The other small boy, seeming to grow tired of urban development, grabbed a large backhoe and joined in as the course of destruction escalated. Within minutes, everyone was laughing, and all five of us were levelling the city with various types of plastic vehicles, buckets and shovels. We exchanged pleasantries, and Logan and I headed off back towards our complex to prepare for the rest of the evening.

I attempted to remove as much sand as possible from every crack and crevice as I had done on so many occasions before when Logan had crossed paths with an inviting sandbox. I stripped him down to everything but his underwear. At almost forty inches he was well above the 97th percentile for height for a two-year-old boy. At twenty-six pounds, the 70th percentile for weight, he was a tall, thin glass of water! I loved to tease him about this. He took off up the stairs in front of me and sprinted all the way to the second floor. I stopped momentarily at the family room on the main floor, just long enough to flash a knowing smile to the other mothers who were starting to congregate there.

Logan was sitting on his cot playing with his small, stuffed elephant when I finally made it to the room.

"How are you doing?"

"I okay! Elephant is Heffalump!" He had always enjoyed Winnie-the-Pooh and all his friends, and even though this elephant bore a resemblance to Heffalump only in the fact that it also had a trunk, it seemed that we had settled on a name.

"Nice! It is time for you to think about getting ready for bed. Mommy is going to meet with all the nice ladies that you met today. You and Heffalump are going to get lots of good sleep in preparation for camp tomorrow."

"No! I with you!"

This was not like Logan. He was always eager to take his blankie and crawl into bed. I dug his well-worn blanket out from the depths of the bottom drawer and offered it to him.

"I with you," he adamantly repeated, meeting my eyes with a demanding glare. He and Heffalump got up from the cot and wandered over to the bottom drawer. He extracted a pull-up and a set of pajamas. He removed his underwear and replaced them with a pull up. He methodically assumed the role of Spiderman with the donning of his newest pair of pajamas purchased specifically for this trip.

"Ready!" he exclaimed, obviously greatly impressed with himself.

I was too tired to argue. I brushed my long blonde hair and my teeth and descended the stairs with a small, blond superhero trailing closely behind me. As I entered the room thinking about what kind of excuse I was going to make, I recognized it was all for naught. Being one of the last to arrive at 9:05 p.m., in atypical fashion, I was met by a room filled with many women, several bottles of wine and children of all sizes and shapes littered amongst the scenery. There was silence for a moment as we entered the room and then a loud chorus of laughter. A smaller woman named June, whose five-year-old daughter, April, was sitting in her lap, rang out, "I see you have also succumbed to the power of coercion."

I threw my head back and drew the back of my left hand across my forehead. "I have!"

Logan and I took our place in the haphazard circle where some were seated on chairs and sofas and some on the floor. The children were, for the most part, serene. They all just wanted to be in the presence of a familiar face on the first night in unfamiliar surroundings. I sat in the one remaining chair and Logan jumped into my lap. I guessed there were no immediate dangers that Spiderman needed to contend with.

Virginia began, "I know that there are small pockets of women here who know each other, perhaps even know each other extremely well, but I think we owe it to each other to dig deeper into each other's lives. We need to find out what more we have in common than just the desire to reproduce on our own. I think we should start with what each of us does to support ourselves in this dream we call single motherhood. Does anyone have any objections?" None of the mothers or children spoke up.

"Why don't you start, Tammy?" she directed toward a short Caucasian woman with curly, greying hair. Tammy had a daughter, Chloe, who was ten years of age. Chloe was one of the few children absent from the room at present.

"I started off in retail after an undergraduate degree in psychology at the local community college. I was working towards my pastry license, on the side, and managed to graduate when Chloe was two. We moved to Santa Fe, New Mexico, when Chloe was three. I had the opportunity to co-manage and be the main pastry chef for a recognized restaurant there. My parents live in Denver, and therefore it was closer to home than Ohio. I love my job, Chloe, and my life. It is difficult, at times. I am sure I don't need to tell this group!"

"Why pastry?" a smaller Nigerian woman, Dayo, with a three-year-old son, Ben, piped up.

"What do you mean why pastry?" Tammy replied with a perplexed look on her face as if no one had ever broached this question with her before.

"I mean..." Dayo hesitated as if looking for the correct words. "I want to know why one does what they do?"

"I knew that I was going to need a job with a good, steady income. I had a friend who told me to do it. He said it was a great job with great hours. I could work wherever and be in demand. I never thought more about it."

The room became silent. I am guessing that we were all contemplating what we were going to say when Dayo's very relevant question was turned back toward each of us in turn. I was sure that each of us had been told to find something that was our passion. I was now wondering how many women in the room found themselves where they were simply by virtue of needing 'a good job', which 'provided a steady income' and may or may not be 'highly portable'.

"Why don't we move on?" Virginia directed to everyone and no one at the same time. She pulled a piece of paper out of her purse and looked down the list. We all waited with trepidation hoping that our name would sink to the background. "Victoria," she said as she looked up and then brought her focus to me. "Why don't you tell us your story?"

I looked up and met the eyes of a room full of expectant

individuals. Logan looked up at me and repeated, "Mommy, your story!"

"My friends call me Tori. I started off with an undergraduate degree in psychology as well," I said looking in the direction of Tammy. "I thought that I was going to go on to complete a Masters, or even a PhD in psychology, however I did not manage to secure funding to continue on after my undergraduate degree. I contemplated my options and settled on applying to medicine."

I knew it was coming. I had always considered my journey to medicine and then on to surgery to be a matter of personal choice rather than a series of fateful events that had led me here. I knew that I was now going to be asked the same questions that Dayo had posed of Tammy, and I was not sure where this was going to lead. Oh well, perhaps this group of women would provide me with greater clarity than I had ever been able to provide for myself.

I looked directly at Dayo. "I was accepted into medical school on my first try. I was at first very excited, however that feeling was quickly followed by 'what the hell have I done'. I have asked myself 'why medicine?' multiple times over the years, as have others. At times, I think that I do have a passion for it, but I am not sure if that passion developed into the path of medicine or whether I have tried to convince myself of that. None of my friends, family or acquaintances remembers me speaking about medicine or wanting to be a doctor before I was accepted into medical school. I do not remember ever wanting to be a doctor, or anything for that matter, as a young child."

I paused and looked around the room. It seemed as

though I had the floor—people of all ages had their attention diverted towards my monologue. Even Logan was looking up at me and pulled on my sleeve as if to urge me to continue.

"I never really thought about what type of physician I was going to become during those early years of medical school. I had always been a good student, and I continued along that trajectory. When I entered my third year, my clinical rotations started, and there became more of a sense of urgency in determining who I was to become. I settled upon psychiatry or family medicine initially as I thought it would fit most with my past exposure in the realm of psychology. I felt most at home in internal medicine, and that was the specialty I eventually applied to. I spent many lonely nights toiling over my applications; nights that were filled with uncertainties and tears. I had even interviewed extensively for a training position in internal medicine when I finally came to my first exposure to Surgery. I went into it as most people who are destined to be internists do—thinking that it would only be a matter of time before I was back amongst the smart people. However, I never looked back." I was starting to speak more quickly now; the excitement I always remembered from that exact moment I knew I was a surgeon was bubbling once again to the surface.

"It was a calm, silent fall day and everything seemed to just settle perfectly into place. I can tell you the exact day, the exact time, and the exact place. We were operating on someone who needed a section of their small intestine removed as it was ravaged with Crohn's disease that was no longer responding to medication. I stared in awe at the inside of the abdomen with all its contents neatly arranged. It was an 'ah ha' moment for me. I knew this was for me. And then I thought, 'oh hell, this is for me!'

"As fate would have it, I alone was not the only one who recognized my passion for surgery. At the end of my rotation as a medical student, some six weeks later, the program director took me aside and told me that they would like me to consider applying to surgery as I was 'just enough of a bitch to fit in'. I decided that I could either accept this as words of encouragement or report him to his superior. I chose the former.

"I have always thought that fate led me to a place where my previously unrecognized passion could begin to be recognized. I had never been exposed to anything like this previously, or since, until Logan arrived, that could ignite my passion. Thus, I was always confused as to whether I became a surgeon by choice or by chance."

I decided that I had told the story as well as I could. I thought it was one of the best renditions that I had ever mustered. Perhaps it was the audience that was allowing me to tell it in as much depth as was necessary to do it justice. Personally, I was no further ahead than I had been previously in deciphering fate from passion, however I decided that this group was going to allow me the perfect opportunity to debate this once again.

Cindy was the first to speak. "I think there is no correct answer here. I will use the example of a woman who finds herself accidently pregnant and decides to keep the baby. We would still refer to her as a single mother by choice even though she did not intentionally set out, from a sense of love or passion or loyalty, to have a child on her own. We do not refer to her as a single mother by chance."

"I see your point," said Teresa. "However, we would still say that it was an accidental pregnancy and that she was a single mother by accident."

"Think of it this way though. If Tori had not had that deep sense of passion and purpose in the operating room that first, fateful day, she would have continued on the path towards internal medicine. It was a conscious decision, spurred on by that day in the operating room and her overall positive, although somewhat unorthodox, evaluation that changed the course of her life," Cindy offered.

Julie, a small Asian woman who had been relatively silent up until this point in time, turned towards Dayo and exclaimed, "I am grateful you ask us to reflect."

The room broke out into a raucous round of laughter. We all agreed that this was a great way to get to know each other. However, it was going to take more than one evening if we were going to spend as much time devoted to each individual as we had spent with my story. We had been there for an hour and a half and had really just completed two stories.

"I am grateful for the time that you have afforded Logan and myself this evening. As a very private person, I know that the value of the gift of listening cannot ever be fully quantified. I appreciate all the comments, especially those you have made, Cindy," I said turning my gaze toward her. "I now firmly believe that being a surgeon was a conscious choice that I made, given my particular circumstances. It arose from a passion that was sparked at a single moment in time and which continues to burn brightly within me. Thank you to all of you!"

The room was silent for only a moment. One person began to clap, followed by another and another, until everyone in the room was engaged. Even those few children who were still awake became engaged in the festivities. We all agreed that this was a great process for getting to know each other and even our own selves better. We agreed that we would start earlier tomorrow night and try to get through at least four people.

I rose from my chair and bundled Logan in my arms. He roused slightly from a deep sleep that had overtaken him about half way though my story. He wrapped his arms around my neck, and the two of us travelled as a single entity up the stairs to our room. I placed him under the blankets on his cot and placed Heffalump beside him. His arms transferred easily from around my neck to a tight embrace of the small stuffed elephant.

I crawled into bed and thought about how fortunate I was. I had chosen my career, and I had chosen my son. How wonderful! That was the last thing I remembered.

24
The Sperm Hits the Egg!

The New England experience was now just a remote and pleasant memory. I had trudged through the tedious nanny selection process once again upon our return from that memorable Single Mothers by Choice vacation and had settled on a recent high school graduate named Melissa. She was a rather thin woman with a pale appearance, shoulder length mousy brown hair and green eyes. Like Lorraine, she seemed to fit the role of a nanny with her appropriate clothes, including well-worn jeans and a simple t-shirt. She also had short, well cared for fingernails. I was not sure what this had to do with being a good nanny, but it remained important to me. The process had been only somewhat easier this time in that there were still only a very few people to select from given the criteria that were demanded from the job. Like Lorraine, Melissa seemed to have a swift and effective affinity for Logan. He understood that she was to be his new nanny and adjusted his behaviour accordingly. While fiercely independent, he knew that he needed to listen to his nanny if we were to sail like a well-seasoned vessel.

We had settled into a successful, but different, new

routine, with remnants of the old and elements of the new. Like Lorraine, Melissa was very independent, and had been known to rearrange entire rooms of the house. Unlike Lorraine, Melissa seemed to be more of a night owl. The routine we had grown into was not distracted by this as she always withdrew to the basement when I was at home. No matter what the challenge, life always had a way of settling people into another routine. I was sure there were those with a much more intricate and elaborate routine, but ours fit the three of us just fine.

I had been intrigued by the fact that some of the women at our fun-filled week in New England had more than one child. One woman in fact had three! At the time, I do not think I was aware that I was watching this subset of women very closely. I was trying to determine what made them more suited to a second child, what made them more courageous and what kind of mental illness a woman must possess to think that this was the kind of thing that should be consciously embarked upon more than once in any given lifetime. I had reflected on this more times than I initially thought I would since the time of that encounter. I was fascinated by the fact that they were not different from myself, they seemed no more courageous in their words or actions, and there did not seem to be any overt signs of a definable mental disease in any of them. Although they represented a small cohort, I was more than a little intrigued.

It was later that following year when I took the plunge. Logan had just celebrated his third birthday the week before, and I was celebrating my forty-second. At first, it had just been a casual conversation with my obstetrician,

Dr. Christine Barkley. However, it soon developed effortlessly into a formal invitation for coffee and eventually into an actual appointment to discuss the logistics of a second child. She was somewhat shocked, and in the beginning tried to gently talk me out of it, or so it seemed. I reminded myself that this was the same woman who, although considered to be a good friend of mine, had tried to suggest that labour would be a good thing to experience during the delivery of my first child. I appreciated what she had to say—with a large grain of salt.

We discussed adoption as an option given the increased risk of congenital anomalies that were possible with advanced maternal age, or as she put it my *very* advanced maternal age. We discussed the very low probability of success and whether we should just resort to medicated cycles. Given the significant chance of a twin pregnancy if I were to choose this latter route of medications to support my fertility, I was able to negotiate for two unmedicated cycles. The first insemination was to take place about two weeks after my forty-second birthday.

I entered her office somewhat apprehensively given the events of my last visit. Once inside, I looked up above the front door and indeed saw the vague outline of the warning — 'Emergency Exit After Hours', now unlit and sitting unnoticed in the daylight hours. I had instructed Dr. Barkley, Christine, that I was not going to allow her to exit the room until the speculum was out. I had also requested a morning appointment to ensure that many hours would need to elapse between the time of the insemination and my need to exit from the clinic.

The process went off without a hitch! Unfortunately,

that was one of the few things that was easy during this pregnancy, which would eventually lead to the birth of my second son, Lucas. I knew from the moment the sperm hit the egg that I was pregnant. It was like a wave of unending nausea that came over me within forty-eight hours of leaving Christine's office. I sat on the couch and wondered what was happening to me. I harkened back to the events of the previous week in order to rule out anything and everything that I might have eaten, anyone who may have been sick around me, or any change in my medications. I was working through the situation like I would for any of my patients whose main complaint was nausea. Then it hit me, like the fury of a betrayed lover. The only thing different in the last seven days was the insemination. I was pregnant! This was certainly the most courageous and the most irresponsible thing that I had ever done!

I called Christine the next morning, three days following the insemination, to inform her that I was pregnant. She laughed and reiterated the unlikely statistics at me. She informed me that it was too early to know and that she would see me for the second insemination in several weeks. I asked her, in the few seconds of silence that fell upon me after her rambling dismissive diatribe, if she would like to know why I thought I was pregnant. It must have been what I said or the way in which I said it that alerted her to the fact that she had not even bothered to ask me why I thought I was pregnant; why I was contacting her so early after the successful insemination. Her response seemed an odd combination somewhere between shame and remorse.

"I am so sorry. Of course, I would like to hear what you

have to say."

"Never mind! I am too tired and too nauseated to carry on this conversation right now. I am sorry that I even bothered you." Before she could even get another syllable in edgewise, I hung up. I reflected on the fact that I was not upset or even angry. I was simply too tired to give a damn. Unfortunately, this was how it was going to continue for most of the rest of my pregnancy.

25

The Fraud Squad

By the middle of December, I was just trying to make it through the five days that I was to have off, at least from my professional life, over the holiday period. I was doing the best that I could to make it through every day of my current pregnancy. Even though I had become reacquainted with my one-year goals, I found myself reverting frequently to my 24-hour list. I was playing the role of surgeon by day, followed by couch potato into the late hours of the evening. Logan was graciously playing the role of three-year-old house butler by bringing me everything I needed to survive while I lay semi-comatose on the couch, fully dressed including my winter coat, night after night. It was another routine borne out of necessity, teaching him responsibility and me dependence in a symbiotic sort of way. He would go to the fridge, and I would instruct him on how to prepare the sandwich de jour. He would deposit my dishes into the sink and crawl up into my lap. We would sit for several hours watching whatever we might fancy on the large, flat screen television. At about 8:00 p.m., I would drag my sorry ass off the couch and deliver Logan and myself to bed. I was frequently not surprised when I awoke in the same clothes, winter coat included, that I had walked through the front door wearing the evening before. Nausea and fatigue were unrelenting visitors.

The few who knew me well knew that I was investing all of the residual energy that this pregnancy would allow into maintaining the façade of surgeon by day. I would sit in the staff lounge between cases and sleep. I took every opportunity I could find to lean against a wall or sleep in my office. I was operating sitting down most of the time, which was somewhat difficult for the bigger cases.

In the midst of all this, I received a call from a pharmacist asking me to approve a prescription for a rather large inventory of narcotics. This had been requested by a supposed patient, written on one of MY restricted prescription pads, with MY signature endorsing this ludicrous transaction. She was contacting me as the patient had not had enough money to cover the cost of his narcotic windfall, and she wanted to make sure I was clear about how much I was ordering. I did not recognize the patient's name, nor for that matter had I ever prescribed the narcotic of record before. She was not surprised. She informed me that the prescription had been accompanied by a second prescription for prednisone. She also informed me that they ensure that they got a picture of his face, when and if he returned. She asked me to go through my restricted prescription pad to see if any of them were missing. She supplied me with the number of the one she had in her possession. I thanked her for the call and hung up.

I retrieved my restricted prescription pad from the side pocket of my briefcase. As I thumbed through it, I noticed that both the original and the carbon copy of the prescription of concern, as well as four others, were missing at random. How clever!

I walked through an average day and who might have access to my briefcase. It almost never left my sight, and my restricted prescription pad had been nowhere else, to my knowledge. A wave of nausea and fatigue came over me, and I decided that this was best left for another day. Besides, the pharmacy would likely be in touch in the next few days to provide me with a more solid idea of who the culprit was. I made a mental note to speak to my boss about further necessary steps.

On December 22, I was in the middle of a busy, pre-holiday clinic when my nurse, Dorothy, rounded the corner into my office. She seemed out of breath, white as a sheet, and initially at a loss for words. None of these were common for her. She managed to blurt out, "There are three cops with guns in the waiting room! They have to talk to you!"

I could not readily think of a single reason why I would be of interest to the three police officers. "I guess you should send them in and bring in another chair please." I wondered what they could possibly want with me. A wave of nausea and fatigue washed over me as I tried to remain awake and calm.

"Dr. Jones?" the first officer inquired as he rounded the door into my office and held out his hand.

"Yes, Dr. Victoria Jones," I rose from my chair to greet him as the two other officers also crowded into my small office. I was relieved that I had put my hair up into a ponytail and that I had decided to wear my wire-rimmed glasses rather than my contact lenses. It would make me appear more professional. I went to button my white lab coat over my favorite black jumpsuit, which I had paired with bright red patent pumps.

I kept the introductions formal as it seemed that the situation was going to warrant that. The fact that all three of the officers were carrying weapons made the room seem even smaller than it normally would with this many people. "I am Lieutenant Randy Steeves, this is Lieutenant Nancy Blackstone and Detective Ricky Peters," the first officer motioned respectively to the two officers standing beside him. "We are from the fraud division of Calgary Police Services."

I looked back and forth across the three of them and asked, "What can I do for you?"

Lieutenant Steeves started the line of questioning. He was almost six-feet tall, like Lieutenant Blackstone, with short blond hair, fair skin and piercing blue eyes. I couldn't help but notice that it looked as if he had been poured directly into his standard issue dark blue uniform. I could feel my heart rate begin to rise as I tried to focus my attention on the issue at hand rather than the distractingly handsome man standing in front of me. "We are here with respect to the narcotic prescription you were allegedly informed about by the pharmacist several days ago. Do you remember that conversation?"

"Of course, I do!" I exclaimed, locking his gaze. "The pharmacist explained to me that they had received a prescription for a large amount of narcotic from a patient whom I had never heard of before. She informed me that she would get back to me when the culprit returned and she was able to provide me with a picture that might allow me to make an identification. I assume that is what you are here?"

I could not discern what thoughts or feelings I was reading from the three of them as they shifted in their places and looked back and forth between one another. I had offered them a seat when they had entered my office, however all three had remained standing. I had chosen not to join them as I thought I might topple over, or worse yet, throw up on one of them. A wave of nausea washed over me. They seemed to be trying to discern who was going to speak next. Lieutenant Steeves, who had initially appeared to be in charge of my interrogation, seemed to be motioning for someone else to take over.

"Sort of," Detective Peters responded, somewhat tentatively. He was about four inches shorter than the other two and dressed in street clothes—a light blue, short-sleeved t-shirt, casual black slacks, and an older pair of Hush Puppies. Unlike the other two, he seemed much more relaxed, perhaps because he did not have a standard issue police officer hat, which needed to be removed and held tightly under his left arm for the duration. "The person of interest returned to the pharmacy yesterday afternoon. They were not able to get an exact identification as the cameras did not capture his face. It appeared that he actually knew where the cameras were located. We suspect that he had staked the place out before."

"So how are you suggesting that we get an idea of who he is and why are you here to see me?" I could sense that the intense blue eyes of Lieutenant Steeves had not shifted from my general direction even though my attention had now been diverted to his partner. I could feel my heart continue to race, not as a result of the interrogation or the temperature in the room, but rather as the result of the continued, unbroken connection that I was feeling between myself and Lieutenant Steeves.

I shifted my focus briefly over to Lieutenant Blackstone, more as a means of trying to determine if I was correct about Lieutenant Steeves. She was tall, almost six feet. Her long black hair fell, without a hint of a curl of a wave, down to the middle of the back of her dark blue, standard issue uniform. Her intense green eyes looked directly out at me from behind her dark brown prescription Oakley eyewear. My instincts had been correct, Lieutenant Steeves had not diverted his gaze from me. I assumed that this was part of his role in the interrogation—to watch closely for any signs of guilt in my behaviour or demeanor.

Detective Peters continued. "The pharmacist provided the person in question with the prednisone. She told him that he would not be able to pick up the narcotic prescription until later in the afternoon as pharmacists do not normally put these together until the payment has been completely finalized. She told him that he should return in several hours. She was able to follow him to the front of the store and get his license plate number. We should note that he was alone in the car."

"So, you were able to identify him?"

"Not exactly," Detective Peters replied.

"So why are you here then?"

"When we ran the license plate through our system, it turns out the car is registered to you!" Lieutenant Steeves proclaimed as I brought my gaze back towards his mesmerizing blue eyes.

"That is impossible! Yesterday afternoon I was in the operating theatre until 4:30 p.m. and no one else has access to my vehicle while I am at work."

Lieutenant Blackstone removed a single black and white photograph of poor quality, but still discernable character, from the inside pocket of her standard issue vest. She showed it to me, however she did not allow me to completely take it over into my possession. Staring back at me was the tail end and the easily recognizable license plate of my nanny's vehicle!

"Is this your vehicle?" she asked.

"Yes, I am the registered owner of that vehicle; however, my nanny is the only person who drives that vehicle." I was extremely confused as to how this vehicle had found itself present and now accounted for at the scene of an unapproved narcotics run.

"Do you know of any male, approximately six feet in height with brown curly hair and a slim to moderate build, who might fit the description of someone whom your nanny might associate with and allow to drive her vehicle?" Lieutenant Steeves inquired.

"Oh my God—I stammered. "You have just described my nanny's boyfriend! You are sure there was no one else in the car?"

"We are confident," Detective Peters replied.

It was all starting to make sense. My nanny's boyfriend, Steve, would have access to my briefcase, which I kept in the front hall at night. He fit the description perfectly, and he had Crohn's disease, a disease for which a number of patients were placed on prednisone.

I looked up in disbelief, and without saying another word looked back and forth between the three looming faces in front of me. I placed my head in my hands, and I thought that I was going to cry—or scream—or throw up—or all three!

"Are we correct in assuming that you knew nothing about this?" Lieutenant Steeves broached somewhat awkwardly. I sensed that I was not the only one feeling the attraction that was mounting between us.

It was at that moment that I realized that the members of the fraud division were not here to seek my input, rather they were here to question my potential involvement in this poorly-timed fiasco. Great, who was going to make my sandwiches in prison? A wave of nausea rushed over me.

"You have a single arrest on your record from several years ago where it was initially thought that you may have been stealing narcotics from a fertility clinic?" Lieutenant Steeves inquired as his face began to go from white to a mild crimson color.

"Oh my God! I assume that you read my file and that you recognize that that was all a huge mix-up?" I could see from the looks on their faces that they were each individually, and probably collectively, intimately familiar with the content of my previous arrest.

"We are aware of the details of your previous arrest and do not feel it has any bearing here. Did you know anything about the current situation?" He was attempting to hold an emotionless face while he questioned me, although I could see the slight glint of an interested smile escaping from below what he wanted me to believe was a hardened surface.

"I can assure you that I knew nothing of this! My nanny is the only one allowed to drive that car—during working hours! She is not to lend it to any stupid friend or any ill-conceived, supposed boyfriend that she might like!"

"We will need to speak with your nanny sometime over the next several days," Detective Peters informed me. "When do you think you will be able to give her some time off? Also, do you know the name and address for your nanny's boyfriend?"

I gave them a first name, Martin. I had no idea of a last name. I told them I would try to think of a way I might be able to track that down. I gave them the address for where I thought he might currently be working. They told me to remain in town and try to keep out of trouble. I reached out to shake Detective Peters hand as the other two officers replaced their hats back on to their respective heads. Lieutenant Blackstone shook my hand in standard fashion. Lieutenant Steeves offered his hand almost too eagerly. Everyone in the room, including Detective Peters, seemed to notice. The handshake lasted longer than the standard one I had received from Lieutenant Blackstone. Again, everyone seemed to notice. I stood to see them off, and as I did so I could feel Lieutenant Steeves edge slightly closer to me, such that he was almost touching my shoulder. While he should have naturally been the first to leave the crowded room, he stood back and motioned for his fellow officers to leave first. This all seemed very awkward, and I thought not the standard way for three officers, especially three armed officers, to leave a small crowded room. He said nothing else to me, but I could sense the heat passing between the two of us as he edged closer to me.

With all the energy I could muster, I winced and asked Dorothy how many more patients were left to be seen. The visit from the fraud squad had taken close to an hour, and I felt a wave of nausea and fatigue come over me.

"I have sent the rest of the patients away, and I brought you a large, piping hot chai tea latte. Merry Christmas and see you in the New Year, Tori." With that, she was gone. You can be damn sure that I am going to have you around the next time the fraud division decides to just drop by for a visit, I thought to myself!

I was hoping that it would not be too long before Lieutenant Steeves contacted me. I certainly would not object to being interrogated by him again!

26

The Silence of a Nanny

During my interrogation by the fraud squad, we had agreed that I would contact my nanny, Melissa, to let her know that I no longer needed her over the Christmas break, effective immediately. The police would contact her the following morning and ask to speak with her. As she was to be working for me, and as she was effectively working for no one else, she should be free to come in and speak with the officers in person. It was a simple, but hopefully effective, plan.

At approximately 6:00 p.m. on the evening of December 23, I received a call from a number I did not recognize. The shrill ring sounded four times before I was able to retrieve my cell phone from its usual place on the counter. Logan looked up from where he was playing contentedly in the middle of the living room floor. As soon as the noise was controlled, he went right back to the issue at hand, the building of an elaborate Lego Village.

"Hello! This is Dr. Victoria Jones."

"This is Lieutenant Steeves from the fraud division. Are you free to speak?"

I glanced over at Logan who seemed oblivious to what

was happening around him. His tall lean body, topped by a mop of blond curls, sat hunched over mountains of unconstructed Lego pieces. He was engrossed in the construction of what appeared to be a containment unit for Lego characters who had run afoul of the law—how appropriate!

"Yes," I replied, my heart starting to race. Again, this had nothing to do with the situation, but everything to do with the man on the other end of the line.

"We were in contact with your nanny, Melissa, earlier this morning. We did not allude to the fact that we had been in contact with you, rather we simply outlined that we wanted to speak with Martin."

"And?"

"Your nanny stated that she did not currently know the whereabouts of said Martin, and that she did not know when she would see him next, if ever. She did not seem upset, in fact she did not even seem surprised that we were contacting her."

"Did she say anything further when you met with her in person?"

"She refused to come in to meet with us. She could not, or would not, provide us with any further information."

I was stunned and embarrassed. I could not fathom a single reason why Melissa would refuse to come forward and at least speak with my acquaintances from the fraud squad. Unless ...

"Do you think that she had anything to do with this?"

"That is what we have been led to believe. There is really no justifiable reason for someone to refuse to speak with us aside from being complicit with the crime."

Multiple thoughts were streaming into my consciousness from all directions. What if Melissa was complicit in this? What had she exposed my son to? Was it possible that she and Logan had been in the car at any point during the multiple trips to the pharmacy? Why did she feel that she would be allowed to let anyone else drive the car, my car? Where the hell was she and what had she done? What had she done? What had she done?!

"What is your next step?" I asked.

"We will contact her again this evening and ask her to appear before us tomorrow morning. If she continues to refuse, we will need to bring her in."

"Do you know where she is?"

"Yes, she is at her mother's house."

We exchanged parting pleasantries and hung up. I had so desperately wanted to speak with him further, however I suspected this would not be acceptable during the course of an active investigation.

Logan and I spent several hours in construction before we shut it down for the evening. I was impressed with the progress we had made on the intricate complex, which was to house illicit Lego criminals. We had managed to pack almost every Lego figure we owned into the structure. I thought about what horrible things these hardened individuals must have committed to find themselves in this predicament.

At approximately 9:00 p.m., we decided to turn in for the evening. It was strange that Melissa had not returned home by this time. I began to wonder if she was going to return at all this evening, or ever for that matter. I sensed that I was headed for another great nanny escapade.

The Silence of a Nanny

At about 3:00 a.m., I was awakened by what I initially thought was someone trying to break into the house. It took me several moments to reflect forward and backward and to settle myself on where I currently resided in time and place. I remembered that I was trying to figure out the complex relationship that had developed between myself and my nanny over the last forty-eight hours. I could faintly see the light from the front hallway making its way underneath my door.

I pushed myself up, grabbed my robe, and made my way to my bedroom door. The blinding light from the hallway pushed its way in as I turned the handle and opened the door. I entered into the hallway and quickly made my way to the kitchen. Standing there, at the sink, with her back to me, was Melissa.

"Hello," I said, somewhat more harshly than I imagined. "What are you doing *home* so late?" I inquired.

"I was out with friends."

"Doing what?" I asked. In all the time I had known Melissa, she had never gone out with friends. I didn't even know if she had any friends. Her life was her work and her boyfriend, her boyfriend and her work.

"Nothing."

"Bullshit!"

She turned to face me, and it looked as if she had cried a river of tears. "What do you mean bullshit?"

"I know everything about what is going on, and I am doing my best to contain myself at this moment." I am sure that Melissa could see and almost feel the trembling of my body, which represented my attempts to hold my intense and potentially explosive emotions in check.

"About what?" she asked rather timidly as she backed up slightly toward the sink.

"About the narcotics, and the use of my car by your so-called boyfriend Martin, and on and on." I replied. I did not think that much more of an explanation was needed or warranted at this point in time.

"Oh ... Right—"

"Why are you refusing to speak with the police?"

We stood there facing one another for what seemed like an eternity. Neither of us seemed to move or to acknowledge, through eye contact or otherwise, that the other was in the room. There was no acknowledgement, that is except for the overwhelming emotion that was encircling the silent space between us. I am sure that both of us were experiencing the same degree of anxiety, fear, confusion, and anger.

"My mother said I don't need to talk with the cops. I know nothing."

I could not believe what I was hearing. "First of all, I think you should know that your refusal to speak with the police has led them to believe that you are complicit in the crimes that Martin has committed." I stopped and looked for either denial or confirmation, and sensing neither I continued, "Secondly, if you were not aware of any of this, are you saying that Martin stole the car? You are aware that you are the only person who was authorized to drive that car."

She was weighing what she was prepared to say next very carefully. If she agreed that she knew nothing, then we would conclude that Martin had stolen the car. If she disagreed, then she would be complicit in at least the fact that she had allowed him to drive the car without my permission. I could sense she was trying to choose the least risky, although not necessarily the most truthful, option.

"I let him take the car."

"What does that mean? I explicitly told you that you were the only one allowed to drive that car. Do you not remember me telling you that?" The rage was developing from a place somewhere deep within me, although I could not tell exactly where. I am sure that she recognized that it was not being well hidden behind my strong, powerful gaze.

"He was out of his meds for his Crohn's disease. He was going to get sick if he didn't get more drugs. You have no idea what it's like for him when …"

"No one except you is allowed to drive that car!" I could feel my face getting red and hot. I recognized that if I did not cool myself down, this was likely not going to end well. Logan was asleep, we were on my home turf, and I didn't have to work tomorrow. To say that I didn't give a crap about how this was going to end was an understatement!

"I know, but he said …"

"He said! He said! What about what I say? You are my employee, and I am your boss! It makes me question every bit of trust I have in you to take care of Logan."

"I love Logan," she stated. She was starting to cry.

"Don't feed me that bullshit! You're just trying to save your sorry ass from me firing you. He committed a crime with that car, a fucking crime, and you won't even speak with the police. For Christ's sake, the fraud squad came to visit me in the middle of a busy clinic! He committed a crime!"

"I love him! I can't turn him over to the cops. I don't know where he is. I haven't seen him in a few days."

"Well, I guess you are going down for him then. If you do not speak with the police and absolve yourself of involvement, you are dismissed on the spot. You will never see or hear from Logan or myself again. You will never be mentioned as having taken part in his life at all."

"I ..., I ..., I can't," she stammered. "You must believe I had nothing to do with this! I would never put Logan in any danger."

"Well, I guess you get to pick between them then," I looked directly into her questioning eyes. "Either you love Logan enough and have enough respect for yourself to do the right thing or you don't. This is not something where you get to win both sides. Either way, it sounds as if you are going to lose something. If you knew nothing of this, then I feel extremely sorry for you, however that is not going to impact on my insistence that you do the right thing."

It was deadly quiet when I stopped. We sat there staring at each other. Neither one of us was crying. Neither one of us was getting out of this unscathed, and neither was Logan. I knew that the outcome of this was going to affect everyone involved. I was not happy about that, but I knew it had to be done. I began to sense, from the passage of time, that she was not going to be able to accomplish what I was asking of her.

"I can't," she finally uttered. She broke her gaze and sank to the floor landing with a muffled thud as her head collapsed into her hands. She looked up at me. "I can't."

"No ... one ... except ... you ... WAS ... allowed ... to ... drive ... that ... car!" I stated placing emphasis on each word, every syllable, especially the 'was'. "I want you out by 7:00 a.m. That will give you about three hours. Leave a forwarding address where I can send your severance cheque. Do not ever approach me for a reference in the future, and do not attempt to contact myself or Logan."

She looked dumbstruck. I am not exactly sure what she thought I was going to say. Certainly, she cannot have expected that this conversation was going to end on a happy note after her refusal to do the right thing. She pushed herself up off the floor and started making her way toward her small living quarters in the basement.

As she walked past me I said, "I would like the car keys right now."

"How am I supposed to move my stuff? You always said that when I was done working for you, the car was mine to keep."

I looked at her in disbelief. I was now the one who was dumbstruck.

"It is none of my business how you move your stuff, and frankly I don't care how you move your stuff. As far as the car goes, I did not think that I had to specify that the car would not be yours if you either committed a crime or were complicit in the commitment of a crime by someone else! If you are too stupid to know that, then you have much more to worry about than just being unemployed and unemployable."

I grabbed the keys from her hand and headed back to bed. I noticed that I had not been fatigued or nauseated during the past hour! Motherhood wasn't as difficult as a surgical residency, but it was sure venturing damn close!

27
Residency and the Question of Motherhood

My mother, Alyssia, had been living with us for about six weeks—since the sudden and unexpected departure of Melissa. It was not quite as hard as I had imagined it was going to be. Logan had made the transition from Melissa to my mother somewhat seamlessly after the first week. With the excitement of Christmas, and the fact that I was home over the holidays, he did not seem to mind. He had asked a few times for 'Mewissa', however seemed to be comforted that Grandma was there to take her place. He had received some new Lego for Christmas, and this was where he was focused.

Dr. Connie Lewiston, one of my favorite residents, had texted me twice in the last twenty-four hours to ask if I had some time to speak. She was similar to me in many respects—focused, goal-driven and with a great vocabulary and a fabulous sense of fashion!

Connie stated that she needed only an hour of my time. I guessed that she wanted to discuss her choice of fellowship, a two-year program of specialization following her General Surgery Residency. While not required, many residents chose fellowships in order to firmly establish themselves as an expert within a certain area of specialization. Connie had been trying to decide between trauma surgery and thoracic surgery, no easy decision given that she was likely to be a superstar in either. We agreed to meet at the Good Earth Café for two reasons—it was always good, and it was nowhere near the hospital! Granted we had never met for coffee outside the hospital previously, but I could sense that this was very exciting news!

As I pulled into the parking lot of the Good Earth, I was already thinking about how the great food and drink was going to be paralleled by great conversation. The final year of residency was very stressful, but also very exhilarating as a new chapter was opening in residents' professional lives. I remembered it to be a very exciting time when I had chosen cancer surgery, Surgical Oncology, as my area of specialization. I had just passed my exams, and thus I was a surgeon. Now I was going to become an expert in the area that I loved the most. It was always exciting for student and mentor when this decision was made.

I did not see Connie. I was looking for a tall, blonde, well-dressed woman of slim stature. There was no one in the place who fit that general description. The shop was decorated with a Valentine's Day theme, a holiday that was just two days away. I knew that Connie preferred a chia tea latte, extra hot, just like myself. Beckoning at me from behind the glass was a fresh batch of white chocolate and blackberry scones. That would do just fine.

I took a seat by the fireplace. I noted that she was already ten minutes late. This was not like Connie, especially when she had been the one to initiate the conversation. I was beginning to worry that something had happened to her when she flew in through the front door bringing the cold winter air along with her. She was wearing a long, pleated beige coat with a long red scarf. She removed her winter apparel to reveal a shocking purple turtleneck sweater and long black slacks tucked into high black boots. Her blonde hair was pulled back tightly, and she was not wearing any makeup. This was unusual for Connie. I also noticed that she looked very drained and sullen for someone who was holding such exciting news. She caught my eye directly and made her way over to where I was seated.

"I am so sorry!" she exclaimed as she took her seat across from me. "I was debating if I should have bothered you, and I just lost track of time."

"What do you mean? I am very excited to hear the good news! I assume that you have made a decision between trauma and thoracic surgery. Well then, which is it to be?"

It seemed as if I had caught her off guard. Her face reddened, and she began to fumble with her cup. She looked down at the table, intentionally diverting her gaze away from mine. She started to tremble, almost imperceptibly at first, and then more pronounced. She looked up at me and the first tear welled up from the corner of her eye.

I passed her a Kleenex, which as Mother of the Year I just happened to have in my purse. "What is wrong?"

"I really don't know where to begin. Maybe I made a mistake in asking to meet with you today. I know that you have a lot on your plate with everything that is going on." It had been difficult keeping the events of my nanny escapades from those closest to me, including colleagues and residents, as they had become used to Logan and Melissa coming by the hospital from time to time for a visit. When they had not been spotted in several weeks, there were a lot of questions. I had decided to be as honest as possible—Melissa did not work or live with us anymore. I had said no more than that, but people knew that my mother was with us until I found a suitable replacement. It had been pushing me toward admitting that motherhood was harder than a surgical residency. I was almost ready to concede.

I did not want to push Connie into telling me anything she was not ready to divulge. At the same time, I wanted to be as helpful as possible in assisting her in working through whatever seemed to be weighing very heavily on her heart and mind. I decided to just sit silently for a moment to see if anything would rise to the surface for her.

"I am at a loss to know what to do, or even what to think. I have been having a very difficult time trying to determine if I am cut out for surgery, excuse the pun!" She smiled ever so slightly.

I stared at her in astonishment. I was expecting to hear about exciting movements forward in her surgical career, and now I was sitting here listening to her contemplate whether she should be a surgeon at all; listening to her question if she had what it takes! I had seen it many times before, of course, as residents neared the end of their training and were trying to figure out what the 'grown up' world was going to hold for them. One could be as brave as they wanted, in the presence of an older more established surgeon, or even a young and inexperienced surgeon, as long as they were not directly responsible for the blood loss, precision of the instruments and ultimately the life of the patient on the table in front of them. I had never thought that Connie would be one of those residents who would be so deeply affected by the transition, especially since she was going to be completing another two years of training and was effectively delaying her entry into the adult world of surgery.

"I am sure that you can do whatever you set your mind to. You are technically excellent, and you have the dedication and passion necessary to carry you forward in this career. I think you—"

"I am sorry, but you are not exactly on the right track. I am indeed questioning my ability to be a surgeon, but it is not so much from the standpoint of my technical abilities, although that is a part of it."

"All right, I give up!" I grabbed my chai and rested back against my chair waiting for the content of our conversation to be divulged.

"I have never understood how you 'do it all'. I have always known that I wanted to be a surgeon and to be married to Frank, however I never wanted children." She put her cup down and stared out the window. I could see that the trembling was returning.

"No one ever said that you needed to have children, to 'have it all' as you put it. You need to decide what is right for you and Frank and go with that, whatever that might be. Why is it such an issue at present? Is Frank telling you that he wants to have children? Is he trying to pressure you into doing something which is not right for you?"

"I'm pregnant!" she blurted out loudly, causing several other customers to divert their attention towards our table. She turned and looked directly at me. "Neither Frank nor I have ever wanted children. We have always been clear on that."

I felt embarrassed that my inquiries had been so off base. I didn't think it was the time to dig deep, or even remain superficial, about how this had come about given what appeared to be the lack of desire, on either the part of Connie or her husband, to have children.

I was feeling more than a little apprehensive about where the conversation should go next. Even though I was the senior partner in this discussion, I felt at a loss to mentor or coach her as I was not exactly clear on what was being asked of me.

"What would you like to discuss?"

"I am not exactly sure. I have been going back and forth on this ever since I found out about two weeks ago. For Frank it is so simple—we never, he never, wanted children. For him, the answer is so simple and straightforward." She looked out the window once again as if she were not expecting an answer, but rather an open forum to let her thoughts and emotions flow. I could definitely provide that.

"And you? You said that neither one of you had ever wanted children."

"I know," she laughed. "It should be so easy, but I am afraid it is not. Ever since I found out that I am pregnant, I have been genuinely excited. I never expected to feel this way as I never wanted children. Frank tells me that it is just because it is something different, a change if you will, in our otherwise *boring* lives." She emphasized the word boring with a slight tinge of sadness and disdain.

"Go on," I prodded.

"Well, there has not been a single day since I found out I was pregnant that I have not wanted to bring this child into the world. I have been afraid to tell anyone else, for many reasons, the strongest of which is that everyone who knows me well knows that I never wanted children. They will think that I am just overcome by a rush of hormones, or something like that."

"What other people think is not really the most pressing issue you are facing right now. What does Frank think, *really think*, about this?"

She placed her head into her hands and just sat there. At first, I thought she was unsure and just biding for time. However, it became swiftly and acutely obvious what Frank was thinking. "Frank will leave me!" she blurted out.

"You don't know that."

"Yes, I do! He tells me so every time I have tried to broach the subject with him. It does not seem to matter that I love him, that I want to build a life with him, or that I seem to deeply want this baby. He wants nothing to do with it. He has told me that I am stupid to even think that this would be feasible without him. He keeps reminding me that we made a pact never to have children and that I have to abide by that pact because I promised him. Otherwise, I am stupid. He feels I am not taking his feelings into consideration. He is set to make partner at his law firm next year, and I have already thrown a wrench into that by wanting to go away for my fellowship. Partners are expected to have their wives present for all firm obligations and events. I have told him I am not a showpiece and that my career is as important as his, but he just claims that I forced him into marrying me and that his mother would never have dreamed of doing this to his father! It infuriates me, but I wonder if he is right. What if all of this is just a means of trapping him more deeply?"

Even though I was still not sure what she wanted from me, at least we were at a point where the information was flowing—flowing like a river towards the ocean after a torrential storm. There was so much there, yet I guessed that we were just scratching the surface. Connie had previously mentioned to me some of the mean and nasty comments that were made by Frank at her expense. I had, on more than one occasion, questioned why she was still with him. She seemed to keep coming back to me for advice, and I was not entirely sure why. I could not advise her on exactly what to do as I had never lived any of this before. In fact, I had not even vaguely experienced anything even remotely similar. I was at a loss for words, although I knew that everything in my being wanted to once again remind her that most of what Frank was saying was not based in fact. I was hoping that the only part that was true was that he would leave her if she kept the baby.

She caught me completely off guard when she turned toward me and asked, "What do you think?"

"What do you mean, what do I think? What do I think about what?"

"About the whole messy thing."

"Let me be honest with you. I am having a difficult time processing everything you are presenting me with. Are you asking me to comment on the pregnancy itself, your abilities as a surgeon, your abilities to balance everything if you choose to go down both paths, or what I think you should do about your complicated relationship with Frank?"

"Any ... and all of it," she replied, once again turning her attention towards the window.

"I hope you don't mind me saying so, but you seem distracted and somewhat aloof about our discussion today. What is going on?"

"I am sorry, but I was very nervous about my meeting with you today. I took something to calm myself down."

"What?" I retorted. "Nothing about this reflects the Connie I know. There is no reason that you should be tentative about approaching me with anything! I recognize that surgery is a difficult path, for all women at times, regardless of what their circumstances are. I am here to try to help you in any way I can. I am not here, however, to tell you what to do. I am here to help you work through the myriad of choices in front of you and to help you to find the solution that is best for you. Can we agree on that?"

"Can't you just tell me what to do?" she retorted, now almost pouting. "You know me, you know my situation, and you know the ups and downs of 'having it all'. I just need to know what to do."

I was staring at her now. It never ceased to amaze me that residents had such a difficult time navigating situations that the remainder of the world might take for granted in the course of their regular lives. I often wondered how residents could make life-changing decisions for their patients yet have no idea what to do when presented with a personal challenge. Maybe most people were like this.

"Let's break this down to try to simplify it. You need to consider all your options, and I can help you do that. We may not reach a decision today, but at least we can get ourselves off to a great start. Can we agree on that?

"I guess," she replied reluctantly and turned her pout towards the window.

"If we are going to do this, I would suggest that sedatives not be part of the discussion in the future. You are a very talented and motivated individual, and I would hate for you to question that fact during this very difficult time in your life. As I have discussed with you previously, being a surgeon means that you hold an unwavering belief in yourself. It is not an ego thing or an overconfident thing, but rather a belief in what you do. What we are about, as surgeons, is benefitting the health of patients and the healthcare system as a whole. I know that you know that."

"I know that," she stated with a sense of historical recognition of our previous discussions around this delicate subject. "I am afraid ..." she trailed off.

"Afraid of what?" I asked, recognizing that any one of the elements alone would be enough to cause a lifetime of apprehension in the best or strongest of individuals.

"Afraid of losing myself," she stated boldly.

It was not a fear of losing her career, or her future child, or even the somewhat questionable relationship with Frank, which she called a marriage. Her fears were a reasonable starting point to our discussion.

"What does that mean?" I prodded further, turning directly to face her and placing my left hand swiftly on her chin in order to redirect her gaze back toward me from the world outside the window.

"I have a vague sense, I think," she stated gingerly. "Before this, I always felt that I was a surgeon; that I was born a surgeon. There were times when I questioned it, especially when Frank and I were pushing against one another in an attempt to define whose career, whose life, was most valuable." She turned directly towards me with her face, body and voice as she continued in a manner that suggested that the ill effects of the sedatives were wearing thin. "I know your thoughts on that, and I have always appreciated them. I love Frank, at least I think I have always loved the idea of Frank and me. However, my most recent predicament has led me to question even that." Once again, she diverted her gaze, this time down towards her cup, which she held tightly between her two talented hands.

With everything in me, I resisted the temptation to comment on Frank. I knew, she knew, we all knew, what I thought about Frank and his attempts to constantly remind her of her supposed position in his battle to be a well-recognized and sought-after lawyer in his firm. This was not ever going to change, at least in my mind. Connie seemed to have a more fervent need to believe it could change if she could just show him how strong she was in her own right. I had never thought he really cared, beyond the ability to say 'my beautiful and attentive wife is a surgeon'.

"Go on," I replied.

"I think about what you have done and how easy you make it seem. I say to myself, that could be me. I think I even believe it for a brief moment, from time to time. I then come back to reality, my reality, and recognize that it is a long distance between the person I know I am and that possibility."

"In what way?"

"I have never imagined myself with children. In thinking about having this child, it changes my whole perception of who I am as a person. I have always imagined the surgery aspect of my life, a life with Frank, but this does not fit the mold."

"Life is not a mold!" I retorted. "Life has a way of winding you around and down different paths that you would never have expected. Our job is to examine these alternative realities, when presented, and to ask ourselves if it is time to consider a different path. That is what is being presented to you now."

"I know that. At least that is what I keep telling myself. I would like my alternative version of reality, as you put it, to be one where there is room for surgery, Frank and this baby. I don't however think that is a viable option."

"Do you know that for sure or are you surmising based on past experience?"

"I pretty well know it for sure. If I push this too far and lose Frank, I do not think that I will be able to survive."

I could not believe what I was hearing! I wondered if she could separate her thoughts and ideas of herself from her vision of herself and Frank. It did not appear so.

"I thought we were speaking about not losing yourself and now we are back to speaking about Frank."

"I know," she sighed.

"I am not going to tell you what to do, and you know my feelings about Frank. I think you should take some time and mull over each of the options and then we can meet again. I think you are really going to have to ask yourself what you can live with and what you can live without.

Besides myself, who else have you told?"

"No one," she replied. "I wanted the decision to be made before I told anyone else."

"I do not believe that is possible. You need to speak with your most valued friends and family members and figure out what they can add to your ability to make the decision that is best for you. Excuse me for saying so, but I think that keeping this between you and Frank is giving you a very unbalanced view about what is possible. You need to ensure that you do not lose yourself in the process. As you said, this is what is most important to you. I appreciate you coming to speak with me today and opening this discussion to others who care about you deeply." I laid my right hand over her left. "Let's arrange to meet in a week or so and explore this further. Would that be all right?"

"Definitely," she replied. "Thanks for meeting with me today."

As we walked out together, I wondered if I had made any positive difference or impact on the course of her future endeavors. I felt uncertain and not encouraged by the way our conversation had gone, although I was unsure as to what could have made it any better.

28
A Change at the Top

The following week, I had my annual performance review with Dr. Christias. By this time, he was well into his second term as the Chair of Surgery and had made it clear that he was not willing to consider a third. Those were not the exact words he had so eloquently chosen when he pulled me aside and indicated that he would be asking each of us to consider an early performance review prior to his stated departure date in six months' time. This fell right in the middle of my second maternity leave. For some of us, like myself, he realized it was not an opportune time as I would be in the middle of seeking promotion. Recognizing that the Chair is always an integral part of this somewhat intense and arduous process, he wanted to ensure that my transition from Assistant to Associate Professor would be as smooth and seamless as possible. There was no way to predict the identity of the next Chair in advance, and thus most of the work would need to be completed by the current Chair in order to try to ensure success, or at least protect from a significant step backward.

There was also the real chance that the next Chair would not be supportive of the work that had already been done on my part. There had been much discussion, mostly gossip, swirling around as to who might be in the running for the role of the next Chair of Surgery. My thoughts ran to thinking about how it was going to be an obvious choice between a few somewhat more or less qualified older white men within the department. I had been involved in many discussions with the other women in my department about whether any of us would ever consider this position—if it were to become available. This conversation always took the same direction. We would start by laughing about the idea that one of us, a woman, would ever be considered for a position such as this. We would then shift towards the more serious dialogue around who would consider the position, aside from the fact that we were unlikely ever to be considered or asked. There were only two of us who would consider it, and I was the most senior! I sensed that these discussions always had more to do with these highly-talented women not believing they could actually take on the responsibilities of this type of position, rather than if they were truly qualified. There were two of us, however, and I had always thought that those were pretty good odds as the five of us got up and walked away from the table. Five of us from amongst one hundred and fifty. I also wondered if the men had the same conversations and exposed themselves to the same self-scrutiny. I highly doubted it.

In preparing for my meeting with Dr. Christias, including discussions with my one-, three-, and five-year goals, I did not have much time to reflect back on the difficult conversation Connie and I had undertaken the previous week. I had texted her saying that I was looking forward to meeting again, having sat for several minutes thinking about whether 'looking forward' was the right phraseology, before sending the message. I had not heard back from her. Logan was also helping me to interview several new nannies, and I was trying to get him prepared for how we were going to do this. Lucas, although still being housed in my protective uterus, was starting to become more active. At least the fatigue and waves of nausea were beginning to subside, or so I thought.

My one-, three-, and five-year goals were concerned and distracted by the upcoming arrival of Lucas. I tried to get them actively involved in the discussion about this important meeting with my boss, however they were more concerned with the anticipated and sustained re-emergence of the 24-hour list following the birth of my second son, Lucas, in about five months. I did not do much to calm their fears, as I could not reassure them that the 24-hour list, which visited only infrequently now, would not be arriving back on the scene for an extended stay with no defined end date.

I entered Dr. Christias' office at 3:30 p.m. on Wednesday afternoon. I had spent the morning fighting with a very difficult tumour. It had refused to let go of its primary place of residence, and not before a vascular and an orthopedic surgeon were present on the scene. My mom had called, at two-thirty, to say that Logan was not feeling well and that she was going to pick him up from preschool. He was apparently asking for me. While this made me proud as a mother, and although I thought that Logan must feel that I am doing an excellent job in this capacity, I felt more tired than I had in several weeks. The nausea was starting to reassert itself. As I walked across the threshold into my performance review, I reminded myself that I just needed to get through the next hour, the next sixty minutes, before I could begin the rest of my day. That was when the real work began—after I left my full-time job!

In the end, I was thankful for the next hour. It took me away from my obligations as a surgeon, a mother, and an impending mother. I was allowed to focus on just myself. It was something I rarely got the chance to do anymore. The conversation centred around who I was as a person, where I saw myself going and how Dr. Christias could help in the transition to the new Chair. Even my one-, three-, and five-year goals seemed reassured. By the end of the sixty minutes, I was reluctant to extract myself as I knew that everything that the rest of the day had in store for me had nothing to do with me. I was only going to be considered as a distant second or even third.

I exited Dr. Christias' office and called my mother. Logan was sleeping soundly and had not thrown up again. Having once been the mother of young children herself, and having also worked full-time, I am sure that she could hear in my voice that I was thankful that I had been afforded a little time. My next call was to the recovery room to ensure that my patient was still doing well. Although there had initially been some concerns, the family were now all gathered around her bedside. I took a few minutes to dress and to visit with my old friend Silence before joining them. The patient and family seemed stable and content. After confirming this with the bedside nurse, I took my exit.

The drive home was peaceful. I reflected on the events

of the last twelve hours and concluded that it had been a successful day overall. I arrived home to find Logan asleep on the couch. As I kneeled down beside him, placing my hand on his forehead, my mother came over and sat in the recliner directly opposite us. She asked how my day had been. The look on her face reflected how I must have looked and felt. I was exhausted. Just then, my pager went off and Logan awakened. I recognized the number of the recovery room. Knowing that this likely meant that I would be needed back at the hospital, I decided to take a few minutes to be a mother, to be only a mother, at least outwardly. Inside, I was wondering what lie ahead for me into the late hours of the evening.

"How are you doing?" I asked, wrapping my arms tightly around Logan.

"OK," he replied groggily. "I feeling better."

"That is good. It must have been very scary for you."

"Grandma came," he turned to smile at my mother, and my heart sank a little. "She made me a comfy bed. She read me a story." He was almost glowing. I hugged him a little tighter.

"I am glad. Mommy was worried about you, but I can see you are doing well."

"Yes, how was your day?" Logan was always like that, more concerned with other people than he was with himself.

"Mommy had a hard day, and I don't think it is over yet. I have to call the hospital to check on a patient. Is that all right with you?"

"Yes!" he beamed.

"I'll be right back," I said as my mother almost

effortlessly assumed my position on the couch and my heart sank a little more.

My pager went off again as I dialed the number that was beckoning me. The clerk answered the phone and stated that Dr. Lewiston was looking for me. I had forgotten that Connie was on call with me tonight, as the senior resident. My thoughts briefly reflected back on our conversation from the preceding week.

"Hello, Dr. Jones," she stated formally. "I think your patient from earlier today is bleeding and needs to go back to the operating theatre. Her blood pressure was $70/40$ and her last hemoglobin was only 66. I have spoken with the OR, and they are holding all the other cases until I have had a chance to speak with you. I have ensured appropriate IV access and also that blood is on hand. If you approve, I will book her urgently and get things rolling. The family was just sent out when I arrived, and I will go and speak with them." She paused and waited for my reply.

"Of course. I will be right in. Have you spoken with anesthesia?"

"Yes, they are aware. I will get consent and have everything ready for when you get here."

"Thank you."

I went back to the family room where Logan and my mother were watching an episode of Blues Clues. They both looked up at me expectantly, knowing what I was going to say next.

I came over to Logan and knelt on the floor beside the couch. I took his hands in mine and said, "Mommy has to go back to the hospital to help a sick patient. The patient needs your mommy right now. Grandma will stay with you. You will likely be asleep by the time that I get home. Mommy loves you very much."

Logan looked directly at me and said, "She is lucky. You are a good doctor. I am lucky." He reached up to hug me and gave me a big Logan kiss. This readily brought tears to my eyes.

As I got up to leave, I thought about how lucky I was. My mother grabbed my hand, squeezed it and told me to take all the time I needed. As I exited the room and was putting on my extra size coat to accommodate Lucas, I looked back at my mother and my oldest son who sat cuddling on the couch. I thought again about how lucky I was, while at the same time my heart sank a little bit more. This was not the first time, nor the last time, that balance meant that motherhood took a back seat to my career. The feeling never got easier, except for the fact that I knew that I was not alone. Mothers throughout time had been repeatedly leaving their children to make the world a better place for all. I was not the exception to this, I was the rule. I smiled softly to myself as I buckled myself up and prepared myself for the rest of the evening.

29

Residency and the Silencing of Motherhood

It was 11:00 p.m. and Connie and I were sitting in the Doctor's Lounge after having returned my patient to the recovery room for a second time. She had been bleeding, and Connie had handled the situation with swiftness and ease. There had really been no role for me, other than the stated rule that the surgeon of note needed to be present in the operating room when the resident was operating. We had finished only a few short minutes ago. Amongst the flurry of activity, my mother had texted to say that Logan was asleep and that I should take my time.

"You handled that very well. I hope you realize that the patient is lucky that you were on call this evening."

"Thank you," she replied in her old familiar voice. "I appreciate you saying that. It is situations like these that reinforce where my talents lie."

I decided not to reopen the conversation we had been engrossed in the previous weekend and were going to be continuing in a few short days. Silence fell between us. I was relieved when she got up first.

"I have some other patients who await me in the

emergency room. I hope we are still on for this weekend?"

"I will be there," I said. With that she was gone.

Logan was his same old self the next day. I did not need to be in at work until 9:00 a.m. for a meeting, and thus I was able to spend some time with him and drive him to preschool. As I left him at the door of the small barnlike enclosure which was his preschool, he gave me a big hug and muttered that I was the best mommy in the world. He said he was very lucky to have me. I marveled at how he sounded like a younger version of myself. He was such a caring and independent young man. My heart rose a little.

The next two days flew by uneventfully. There were snippets of idle gossip about who might be the next Chair of Surgery, but really nothing one could sink their teeth into. Logan was good, Lucas was good, my mother was good, and all was good with the world.

My meeting with Connie almost snuck up on me. I entered the Good Earth at exactly 9:55 a.m. on Saturday morning to find Connie already there. She had ordered us steaming hot chai tea lattes, just the way I liked them.

As I sat down, I noticed that she seemed more serene and calm, rather than medically sedated as she had been at our previous meeting. It seemed to me as if she had made some decisions and that she was satisfied with her current situation. I anticipated that she was coming to terms with how she might feel about being a mother and how her life was going to move forward without losing herself in the process.

"Thank you for meeting with me again. I know you are very busy and that you had to come in unexpectedly on Wednesday night. How is your patient doing?"

"Very well," I replied. "It does not seem that the second trip back to the OR is affecting her postoperative course. I am thankful that you were there to help her that evening."

"You're welcome. Always a pleasure to help someone you look up to and admire," she said looking directly at me. Again, I noted a certain calm that had been missing previously.

"How are you doing?" I inquired.

"Very well! I took your advice and sat down with all the options in front of me. I explored each option and what each would mean for me and my future. I tried to focus on what was best for me and not anyone else. I took some time with each option trying to visualize what a future with that option might look like. It helped me to make some very important decisions."

"Go ahead," I said, offering her the floor. I was eager to hear about her progress.

"The options, as I see them, include various combinations of a surgical career, potentially motherhood, and either being with or without Frank. I wrote all of these combinations down and worked my way through them one by one. The easiest was the decision that I need to be a surgeon. As you could see from Wednesday night, I am good at what I do. I deserve to be a surgeon. It is who I am. Heck, I think that future patients will benefit more from having me as a surgeon than not!" she exclaimed.

I was relieved to hear that Frank had not made it to the top of the list. Although I had not had much time to reflect on our previous conversation, I was worried that she might somehow conclude that Frank himself, or her vision of them as a couple, would take precedence over her future career or potential offspring. This did not appear to be the case. I looked over at Connie and motioned with my right hand that she should go on.

"I have also made the decision that I am going to accept a fellowship in trauma surgery. It is the excitement and the complex nature of these types of patients that I enjoy the most. There is so much room for advancement and development in this area, and I want to be at the forefront. I am hoping that you will support me in this."

"Of course! I think, as we have discussed previously, that you will be a phenomenal trauma surgeon. You have a lot to offer future patients, trainees and the system of trauma as a whole. I am happy for you, happy that you were able to make the decision during this very difficult time."

It seemed as if my last comment had brought her back to her present reality, rather than any vision she might have of herself as a future successful trauma surgeon. Her demeanor became somewhat troubled, in what way I could not exactly say, just that it seemed to become different and not as positive.

"Yes, the options that presented themselves after that initial decision was made were not as easy or forthcoming. I felt uncomfortable reaching out to others."

"It seems as if you have at least made some progress. Any thoughts on where you might go next in your deliberations?"

She was quiet for a moment and turned her gaze once again to look out the window. I wondered what was troubling her the most, the potential baby or her relationship with Frank. I decided to start with the latter.

"Have you made any headway into your relationship with Frank and where it factors in all of this?"

"I love Frank," she replied, almost deliberately and somewhat defensively.

"I know. You have told me that many times, and I believe that you do have strong feelings for him."

"They are not just *strong feelings*," she retorted. "I love him very much."

"I know," I repeated. "I am getting the sense that I have done something to offend you. Is that the case?"

"Not exactly. He just reminded me that you do not like him very much and that all discussions with you are going to be clouded by that fact."

I could see where this was going, and I was uncomfortable. By choosing not to bring others into the conversation, she had basically limited her discussions to Frank and myself, two very different individuals who did not like or respect each other very much. I felt like this was going to be a tug of war between what Frank wanted and what I thought. I reminded myself that I was here only as a sounding board; I was not here to hand over the final decision to her as she seemed to desperately desire.

"I would like to make one thing clear. I am here to offer support and to act as a sounding board for what your future holds. While it is true that I don't like Frank very much, any decision that you make has to be what is best for you, whether that includes Frank or not. I am not the one who will need to look back on the decision and wonder whether it was the right one or not. That will be you, and you alone. Hopefully, when you look back you won't wonder whether it was the right decision or not. Hopefully, you will put in enough effort up front to know it was the right decision for you."

She seemed to have softened somewhat. I was unsure where she seemed to get the idea that I was expecting a particular decision from her and that failure to come to that conclusion was going to be met with some kind of retaliation on my part. Perhaps this was what Frank had been telling her, but I was not going down that road.

She turned to look out the window again. I could see that something was continuing to trouble her. I knew it could not be easy for her, but there was something else ...

"I have made my decision," she said, bringing her gaze back in line with my own. "Go on," I urged. I surmised that her decision was that she was either going to leave Frank or that she was going to leave this baby. I did not think that the decision spoke to a future where there was room for everyone. I wondered about how she had made the decision or how the decision had been made for her.

"I have decided that there is no room for a child in my future right now. Frank has helped me see that. I will not have enough time and effort to expend on my career, his career and a baby."

"Is this you speaking or is it Frank?"

"We are both in agreement."

"What about your thoughts from last weekend when you spoke of wanting this child and a future that included this child?"

"I don't think that was me speaking. I have never wanted children and Frank has helped me see that I was only temporarily being drawn into this foolish idea by a flurry of hormones and ideas about how great it might be if—"

I raised my right hand and interjected it between us. "I remind you that this is not about Frank! This is about you!"

"Leave me alone, just leave me alone! This had nothing to do with you. It is obvious that you have your heart set on me being just like you—alone and without anyone to help you raise your child. This may work for you, but it will not work for me!" She was now crying, yelling and trembling in unison.

I reached across the table and forcibly extracted her hands from her face where they had come to reside at the conclusion of her accusatory diatribe. I brought her hands down to the table. I looked directly at her and asked in as calm a voice as I could muster, "What is going on here?"

"I cannot be you! I don't want to be you!" she stated, returning my gaze.

"This is not about me! This is about you! I don't know whatever gave you the idea that I wanted, or expected, you to be like me. I want you to do what is right for you. This is not easy, and regardless of your decision, there will be times when you will look back and question it. I want you to make the decision that has you looking back the least number of times and with the least number of regrets. You cannot get out of something like this unscathed."

"Frank said that you just wanted surgeons, female surgeons, who could be exactly like you."

"I would hope that you would know that that is not true!" I exclaimed, recognizing that I should have guessed where this was coming from.

"I am so confused." She removed her hands from my grasp and brought them back up to her face. She started to cry once again.

"I know," I offered.

"What have I done? What have I done?"

"What do you mean?"

"I have already had an abortion. Frank and I went to the clinic on Thursday when I was post call. I knew that I could not have both Frank and a baby. I have chosen to keep things the way they are as I head into a difficult fellowship. Frank knows that this is what is best for us."

I did not interrupt her this time. Rather, I stared in disbelief. In the end, she had allowed Frank to determine what was best for them, for her. She had made her decision; the decision to silence that small voice inside of her that was urging her toward motherhood. I thought about the fact that we had worked together on Wednesday night, less than twenty-four hours before the procedure that would change the direction of the rest of her life. She must have purposefully kept this information to herself to make it to the next day without having to explain her logic.

"You must hate me for what I have done?" she inquired.

"I do not hate you, and this is not about me. All I want is what is best for you. You have made your decision based on what you feel is right for you. I support you in this. I am glad that you have come through the procedure without any complications. I am sure that none of this has been easy for you. I hope that you will be able to look back and know that this has been the right decision.

"I hope so too," she replied with a slight degree of hesitancy, "I hope so."

I think we both knew, as we sat there with Silence, that she would reflect back on this many times and with a mix of emotions. This was just the beginning of a very difficult journey.

30
Remorse

I had thought about Connie a lot over the last four weeks since our last meeting, more so in the first few days. I wondered if she had truly made the decision that was right for her. I had heard that she had taken about a week off shortly after we had met, and I had sent her a text stating that I hoped she was doing all right and that I was free to speak if she needed me. I had heard nothing in reply. When Silence behaved in this manner it made me sad. I questioned whether I had done enough.

Logan and I had been lucky in welcoming a new nanny. My best friend, Rosalee Crookman, was looking to give up her nanny, Audrey, and did not want her to be left without employment. Audrey came with a solid reference from Rosalee, and she was ready to start immediately. I knew Audrey from previous interactions and playdates that Logan had had with Suzie, Rosalee's daughter. Rosalee travelled extensively with her work as the CEO of a multinational corporation, and she was leaving once again for about a year. Her husband, Rick Wiley, was going to be able to take some time off work to look after five-year-old Suzie. Everyone was ecstatic about the whole situation.

Rosalee had not been present at Logan's birth as she had been outside the country. She had made it a prerequisite of her new job that she was not able to leave until after the birth of Lucas. I had informed Rosalee that if I agreed to hire Audrey, and I understood that I was getting the better end of the deal, that it would be for the long term. I was not willing to consider a short-term position. Rosalee had graciously agreed. She knew that I was dragging my heels on finding a new nanny after the issues that had arisen with my most recent nanny, Melissa. Melissa's boyfriend, Martin, had been stealing my narcotic prescriptions and was wanted by the fraud division of the local precinct. Melissa had refused to speak with the police until such time as it had become apparent that Martin was wanted in several other jurisdictions, in several other provinces, for the same type of fraudulent behaviour. I had heard, through the grapevine, that it wasn't until she found out Martin also had a wife and a young son who had been looking for him, that she agreed to speak with the police. Martin was in a court-mandated drug and substance abuse program in British Columbia, about a ten-minute drive from my parent's house near Victoria, awaiting decisions regarding alimony and child support for his wife and son who resided in Phoenix, Arizona. I did not specifically know or care where Melissa was.

Audrey moved in with us in early May, about two months before Lucas was set to arrive on the scene. Unlike my first pregnancy, this one had been more difficult, from the moment that the sperm hit the egg. Even though the fatigue and nausea had seemed to subside over time, I had been doing most of my operating in a seated position.

This was not always easy when one was grappling with an unrelenting tumour whose weight was well into the double digits.

My mother, Alyssia, was staying on with us until after Lucas was born. My father, Willard, was going to be joining us in about two weeks. As Logan had been delivered by emergency C-section and seeing as both of my parents had missed the blessed event, they wanted to be close by for the encore. Lucas was scheduled to be delivered by elective C-section three weeks prior to his due date, the estimated date of confinement, or EDC. I had always thought this was a very primitive way to refer to such a joyous occasion. It seemed to linger from a different place in history, having managed to stand the test of time. Dr. Christine Barkley, my obstetrician and close friend, knew better than to try to discuss the potential benefits of vaginal birth after Caesarean section, or VBAC. During my first pregnancy and delivery, I had been deluded into a false sense of security about the benefits of a 'natural' delivery. We all knew how that had turned out! I was not about to be regaled on the potential benefits of VBAC!

An easy and respectful relationship had been developing between my mother, Audrey and myself. My mother was very familiar with my open approach to motherhood and the expectation I had for my nannies that they were to think of themselves as a primary caregiver. If something went wrong, they were expected to have a plan; they were expected to deal with almost anything. This was the way I treated my residents and my oldest son, Logan, as well.

About a week before the scheduled C-section, I got a cryptic message from Connie asking if I could speak with her and declaring it was urgent. At first, I thought that this was not like Connie. However, I was not certain I knew what was going on with her anymore. Does anyone really know what is truly going on in anyone else's life?

I looked through my busy schedule and settled on some time the upcoming Monday morning at 7:00 a.m. I instructed her that we would meet at the hospital and that I had another meeting at 7:30 a.m. sharp. She readily accepted. I was going to try to pull this relationship back to a more formal position where I was in charge, if that were even possible. Having the conversation in my office was the first step in attempting to do this.

I arrived to find her sitting outside my office. We had not seen each other in quite some time and we both stared at each other in disbelief at how the other person had changed. Her eyes focused on my ever-expanding abdomen, and my gaze settled on her neck which was devoid of the large glaring diamond wedding and engagement duo which she usually wore on a secure gold chain. She looked calm and sure of herself with mostly reflections of the Connie that I used to know. I knew that she had just passed her exams and was set to move to Atlanta for her fellowship in the next several weeks. I wondered how that reality was settling in for her and Frank.

I invited her into my office, and we each took a familiar seat. I remembered that most of our discussions about her professional and personal life had taken place in this environment. The last two encounters were not the more familiar ones, although the intensity of the conversation had made them seem more common or more familiar.

"Thank you for meeting with me this morning. I will

not take up much of your time. I wanted to thank you for everything you have done, and everything you have tried to do, during my time as a resident." She reached into her purse and pulled out three small packages, which she set in front of me. "There is one for you, one for Logan and one for Lucas. The one for you has this card." She removed a bright yellow envelope from her purse. I was beginning to wonder what else she had in there.

I opened the card slowly. On the front was the picture of an old turtle crossing a bright, solid white line. There was a sign beside the line, which read in bright orange letters 'FINISH LINE'. I opened it to reveal the simple caption 'Slow and steady wins the race'. Written below this, in familiar handwriting, was the following:

Thank you for everything you have taught me and everything you have given me, especially the belief in myself. I will remember this always. Connie.

"Thank you," I said. "You didn't have to do this."

"You and I both know that I had to do this! This is not an easy journey for anyone, and you have helped make it a little easier for me. You have forced me to believe in myself, even when no one else did. That is something that is hard for me to do, to keep doing, especially when everything is piling up against me."

"Frank believes in you," I offered, even though it hurt the deepest reaches of my very being. I knew that this needed to be said as she ventured forth into the next chapter of her interesting life.

"I left Frank. After we last spoke some weeks ago, I kept reflecting back on what you said when I asked if you hated me for what I had done. You took the question in stride, knew that it came from a place of deep emotion, and said that you were all right with whatever I decided. I realized shortly thereafter that in the two conversations I was holding, the one with Frank and the one with yourself, there was only one person who was willing to be there no matter what, even as I pushed you aside."

I stared in disbelief. Connie was far more complex, and far more secure in herself, than I had realized. A small smile came to my face.

She continued as if she needed to put it all on the table before someone stopped her, "I apologize if I disrespected you. I meant to come and speak with you earlier, however I wound up in the hospital with a significant postoperative infection following the abortion." She turned away from me now, and I sensed that she was longing for the window she had stared out of some time ago at the Good Earth Café.

"The gynecologist I was admitted under, Dr. Barkley, told me that she knew you very well. She explained to Frank and me that it was a severe infection, that she was sorry, and that she thought there was a high chance that I would not be able to have children in the future." At this point Connie hung her head in her hands.

"Do you know what Frank had the audacity to say right then and there, in front of Dr. Barkley?" she asked rhetorically. "Thank God for that! We never have to worry again about a baby potentially ruining our lives. It is what we both wanted. This is wonderful news."

I could tell by her tone that this had not been wonderful news for her. I waited to see if there was anything else she wanted to say.

Remorse

"I realized then and there that he always speaks for me. Even though I had discussed my feelings about this pregnancy and the remorse I felt for the loss of the child and the way I treated you, it never seemed to impact him. He never swayed from what he thought was the best for both of us. No, actually what was the best for him. Even on the day I left, about a week ago, the last thing he shouted at my back as I crossed the threshold was that we never wanted children and how could I ruin his career! There was never any consideration of my thoughts or feelings. Two days later, he texted me about an event, which is to be taking place this upcoming Friday. He stated that he expects me to be there to support him. He said that we would tell everyone that I was going to Atlanta for two years and that I would then return to Calgary where I was going to be practicing as a full-time trauma surgeon. He sent seventeen texts to the same effect. I met last Friday with Dr. Jamison, the Program Director, as I know that you trust him. I told him everything. I wanted him to know that if I were to be hired back, it would be on my own merits. He sat and listened and then offered support, much like you have always done. Frank thinks I am leaving in two weeks. Dr. Jamison agreed that I will leave tomorrow as I am afraid that things will escalate once I am not in attendance for the Friday evening soiree. I came to say thank you, to say good-bye, but also to make you aware that I am not sure what Frank might do. He has not mentioned you specifically, but he knows that you were the only other person with whom I spoke."

I was speechless! I was not afraid of Frank, that part did not concern me. I was amazed with how strong the human spirit could be when it needed to be.

"If I ever have the opportunity to have children, although I think there will be a slim chance of that now, I will think of you and the way you graciously conduct yourself as both a surgeon and a mother. I hope you do not mind if I keep in touch."

"Certainly not! I would most definitely appreciate that."

There was a knock at the door. I got up to open the door for my 7:30 appointment who was right on time. Connie got up and excused herself, not familiar with my accountant who had agreed to an early morning meeting. I thanked Connie for coming, we hugged, and she left. I knew that life would offer her some very interesting opportunities. I knew that she would be all right.

31

To Dance with a Psychopath

At about 7:30 p.m. that same Friday evening, I received a call from the hospital operator that a Mr. Frank Sango was looking for me and that I knew who he was. I was perplexed for a few minutes, and then it dawned on me that Frank was Connie's husband! I didn't think that I had heard his full name more than a handful of times, but I was pretty sure this was who it was. At about 8:30 p.m. the operator called again and stated that this was the seventh call in the last hour. What should she be telling him? I asked that she put him through to my cell the next time he called. I gave explicit instructions not to give him my cell number, but rather to just put him through.

I did not have to wait long. Approximately four minutes later, my cell phone rang. I waited for the fifth ring so as to not seem too eager or too fearful.

"Dr. Victoria Jones speaking."

"This is Frank Sango! Where is Connie?"

"I am sorry. Who is this?" I was not going to offer him the benefit of thinking that I knew who he was or that I might be expecting his call. Two could play at this psychopathic game.

"Frank Sango, Connie Sango's husband."

"I am sorry, but I do not know anyone by the name of Connie Sango. You must have the wrong number. I can put you back in ..."

"Connie Lewiston, you bitch!" he screamed at me through the startled phone line.

"Ah yes," I said, deliberately holding steady the calibre and tone of my voice. "Great resident!"

"Where the hell is she, you bitch?"

"I am sure I do not know. I am not her significant other. Perhaps you should check with him. Oh, that's right—that would be you! No use then, is there?" A satisfying smile spread across my face.

"I know that you know where she is! She agreed to attend a function for my firm this evening. I am getting worried about her. Do you have any idea where I might be able to find her?" The tone of his voice had softened and taken a more inquisitive rather than a demanding tone. *He is good, very good,* I thought!

"I don't know where she is. I have not seen or heard from her in several months. The last I heard, the two of you were getting ready to move to Atlanta at the end of the month." I reminded myself that anything which had been divulged in the last meeting in my office, between Connie and myself, was off limits in this conversation. I had dealt with psychopaths before, in fact I had read extensively about them after the dreadful ending of my last relationship. The tone of this conversation, moving from an angry and demanding position to a charmed and soothing demeanor, was all too familiar to me. I was getting ready for the expected escalation back to anger as the conversation continued and he felt I was not willing to deliver what he wanted.

"I am not moving to Atlanta and neither is Connie! She is staying right here in Calgary!"

"I was not aware that she had been offered a job in Calgary." It would appear that Frank was more deluded than I originally thought.

"She will not be working outside the home!" he yelled at me. "I know that she told you she was pregnant and that she was planning to quit surgery, become a full-time mother and support me in my career. It is very important to the other members of my firm that each partner have a dedicated wife, and children, to support them."

Now I was confused. It would appear as if Frank thought that Connie was still pregnant and that she was going to remain with him! This did not fit the storyline that I had been offered by Connie where neither one of them wanted children. I reflected on how far I could safely go in this conversation without getting myself into trouble.

"Connie told me that neither of you ever wanted any children." I decided to leave the part about trying to decide what to do with the current pregnancy out of the conversation.

"I don't want children! I do not know or care what Connie wants! Children are required by the firm and Connie knows that. We had been trying to get pregnant for a while and now we were getting close to fulfilling all my dreams."

"Then I am sure she will be back in touch with you soon. When was the last time that you saw her?" Everything in me wanted to scream 'what about her dreams?' I knew, having been in similar situations and having meticulously extracted myself from them, that it was unlikely that he would even understand the question.

There was silence on the other end of the line. The conversation with a psychopath was a constant dance. Two steps forward and one step back, over and over again. I had learned that the only way to stay on top was to remain calm and feed it back as good as the lunatic on the other end of the conversation could dish it out.

"Yesterday morning before she left for work. She was going to spend the day getting ready for this evening. We were going to meet here at 7:00 p.m.," he stated precisely.

I texted Connie, 'I have Frank on the line. He insists that you are keeping the baby and that you are quitting surgery—please advise'. Even though I knew how to text, and did it frequently, I was from a generation that believed that one should inquire or respond in full and grammatically correct sentences.

"Perhaps she is just late. Anyways, I don't know why you are calling me. I have not seen or heard from Connie in months.

"I don't believe you."

Now it was my turn to be silent. He was obviously better versed as a psychopath than I was, and I needed time to mentally check that all my facts were adding up. I was even regretting that I had just texted Connie as a reply would only add to the degree of mental gymnastics I was needing to perform. Just as I was lamenting my last move, a text came through. It was from Connie.

Frank is psychopath. Verbally and physically abusive. Abortion my idea.

This was followed shortly by another text:
Now want children. Not with him.

This did not really help or hinder my discussion with Frank. I had known that he was a psychopath and verbally abusive. I had surmised a long time ago that he was likely physically abusive, and within the last few minutes, that the abortion was her idea. I knew that she now wanted children, and it followed from everything above that she did not want them with Frank.

"It does not matter what you believe. You are harassing me, and I will have none of it!" I abruptly hung up the phone. I knew the only way to achieve resolution when one got into this type of a situation with a psychopath was to ignore them totally. Any type of attention would escalate the situation.

I called the switchboard and told them I was not accepting any more calls this evening. I then called security at the hospital and alerted them to what was going on. I was thankful that Frank had never been to my house, with Connie, for any of the resident events. That was beneath him. I was betting that he was regretting that now.

A few minutes later my pager went off, and I recognized the familiar number of the hospital switchboard. Following my conversation with Frank, during which time Logan had been contentedly distracted by an episode of The Backyardigans, I had descended the stairs to Audrey's living quarters and asked her to come and take Logan for an ice cream cone and to keep him out of the house for an hour or so in case Frank called back. Luckily, my mother and father were out with a bunch of recently acquired friends for the evening.

I dialed the all too familiar number and announced to the operator that it was Dr. Victoria Jones. She replied that she had Dr. Connie Lewiston on the line. She inquired as to whether she could put her through to my cell phone.

"Most definitely!"

Almost immediately, my cell phone rang. I picked it up on the first ring, "Dr. Victoria Jones."

"This is Connie. I thought that I should probably give you a call."

"Yes, I am somewhat confused as to what is going on here."

"I know you are probably busy so I won't keep you for long."

"Go ahead."

"I will begin with some background about what has been going on over the past several years. I think I need to lay all my cards on the table."

"I would think so," I replied.

"Things have not been good between Frank and myself for a very long time. The abuse, mostly verbal at first, I think you know about from what I previously told you. The physical abuse started almost two years ago. As with the verbal abuse, I was shocked at first, but then I grew accustomed to it. As it continued to escalate, I was unsure as to what I should do. I was not sure who would believe me, but mostly I was embarrassed about how someone in my position could allow this to happen to themselves. I was, after all, supposedly a smart, very well educated and very well put together woman. The divide between my professional and my personal life was becoming deeper and deeper, and I did not know where to turn. Neither Frank nor I had ever wanted any children, and it wasn't until there were rumblings from him that the partners were expecting children, and direct confrontations between myself and some of the other wives regarding this issue, that I knew I could not skirt it forever. In fact, Frank's boss personally took me aside at an annual event held by the firm six months ago and instructed me that they were all expecting that children would be arriving on the scene and that I would be giving up my hobby of surgery. He instructed me that this needed to happen before Frank would even be considered for partner. I could not believe what I was hearing."

Nothing to do with this story was shocking to me anymore. I had been living with the disbelief and complex stories and lies of this situation for what seemed like such a long time now. I was ready to believe anything. I was hoping that this time the story would lend itself to the truth, the whole truth and nothing but the truth.

"Are you still there?" she asked.

"Yes," I replied. "You will have to excuse me if I seem a bit distant. I am trying to convince myself that what I am hearing, this time, is the complete and honest truth. Certainly, you must understand that I have reservations?"

"I have nowhere to go now except the truth."

"I hope so. My ability to listen and to try to help you is wearing thin."

"I understand. I am also getting tired of incomplete truths and delicately placed words. Shall I continue?"

"Yes."

"I left Frank, on two separate occasions, starting about two years ago with the onset of the first physical violence. He was always so charming when we were not together. The fact that I really did not want to fail at this marriage thing led me back to him both times. When his boss approached me last Christmas, I lamented that I was either in, and my marriage was a success, or I was out and I was a failure. I decided that I was all in."

I was always astonished by how much successful women, and I guessed successful men for that matter, felt that success could never be fully achieved if there was even the slightest suggestion of failure. They even came to define certain things that are almost the norm in society, such as the high rate of divorce, as failure. I had felt the same way prior to my first significant defeat. However, I had befriended Failure on so many occasions that he was now starting to gain the same familiarity that I had always had with my good friend Silence.

"More than a few months ago, I found out I was pregnant. Frank was ecstatic that he was well on his way to becoming partner and had even offered to write my letter of resignation. I told him that I had no intention of resigning from the residency and that I was even contemplating a fellowship. I think this made him extremely anxious, more so the part about completing residency because then he knew I would be able to practice as a surgeon. He did not want that. His behaviour became even more erratic and abusive. As the pregnancy progressed, however, a funny thing happened. I realized that I enjoyed being pregnant, and I was actually looking forward to welcoming the baby. I did not care about the abuse anymore. By this time, Frank had cut me off from virtually all my friends and family. Work was my only refuge. He insisted that I needed to tell the world, and I refused to tell anyone.

He insisted that he was going to make my life a living hell if I continued to refuse. I offered that things could not get much worse. That was when I decided to leave for good. However, I also knew if I had this baby, whether here or somewhere else, that I would always be tied to Frank in some manner. I could not bear the thought of that."

"When I met with you the first time," she continued, "my intention was that I was going to tell you everything. When I told you about wanting children, however, I didn't think that you would understand that I did not want this particular child. My feelings of failure began to creep back in, and I made you believe that I had still not made up my mind about what I was going to do. The abortion was already scheduled for that Thursday, and I had every intention of going through with it. When we were forced to work together that Wednesday evening, I knew that I had to keep it all business. You were impressed with my handling of the situation, mostly I think because I was so focused, I had to remain so focused, in order that I not come out from behind my façade. I was afraid that you would try to talk me out of things, that you would tell me that anything was possible. It was not until two days later when you basically said you would support me, no matter what, that I began to realize that you would have understood. When I lashed out at you that day, I think it was more about how frustrated I was with myself. After that meeting, I did not know if I was ever going to be able to face you again."

"Go on," I encouraged. The momentum of her iteration of the events seemed unending.

"I knew that I had to face you, and that I had to thank

you for what you had done for me. I had to provide you with some form of warning against Frank. I knew the fury behind his dream of partner and that he might lash out at others if he could not get through to me. I even told him that I had miscarried, before I left for Atlanta, as I wanted that emotion to be directed at myself only. If I know Frank, he will probably behave as if I am still pregnant in order to try to get you to open up and state that you know more than you do. You should go along with what he says, but please don't let him know I am already in Atlanta. That is more for your sake, than mine, as then he will know that you have spoken with me." She was reinforcing what I already knew, that the events of our last meeting in my office could never come to light.

"The best thing for you to do is to ignore him," she stated. "Do not give him even the least bit of recognition or his behaviour will escalate."

"I know that all too well. This conversation never happened. Take care of yourself and maybe someday we will speak again."

"I would like that," she stated as the line went cold.

Frank called the switchboard operator numerous times that evening, but to no avail. After about thirty attempts to reach me, with various types of aliases, security told him that they would need to inform the police about his behaviour. This seemed to put an abrupt end to everything. Given his past history, I was confident that this was not his first, or his last, brush with the law.

32

Lucas

Three days later, Lucas arrived. It was as simple as that.

I awoke on Monday morning at 5:30 a.m. Logan was already awake and excited as he was going to be a big brother, and he was going to get to spend the day at the hospital with Grandma and Grandpa.

Rosalee arrived to pick us up at 6:30 a.m. We were all standing at the front door. Everyone piled into her minivan—me in the front seat, Logan in the back with Audrey, and my parents in the intervening row. We buckled up in preparation for the day.

The ride to the hospital was an uneventful one. I thought about how many times I had taken the same familiar route previously. This time I was not to be the physician of record, I was to be the patient. I found this to be quite unnerving. I think every physician is quite reticent to seek medical attention, especially if it is in an area with which they have great familiarity. I had spent many weeks after my first Caesarean section concerned that my perfectly placed incision would rip open, likely at the most inopportune time, and my guts would spill out onto the floor in front of me. Of course, that had never happened, however that did not mean that it was not a significant and real possibility this time!

Rosalee rounded the corner and headed toward the parking lot. We had been making small talk, mostly about our respective children and her impending sabbatical to the United Kingdom. I had looked back on several occasions to see Logan beaming in recognition of the fact that we were talking about him. We passed into the parking structure and drove up to the third floor before we were able to find a parking spot.

We all piled out of the minivan. Rosalee asked Logan how he felt about becoming a big brother. He said he was very excited that there was going to be another kid around the house. Like all older siblings, I do not think he fully understood the gravity and permanence of the situation.

We presented to the labour and delivery floor in the North Tower, third level. They had been awaiting my arrival. As we were checking in, another familiar face came down the hallway. Cynthia, who had been present at my first delivery, had been invited by Rosalee and given special permission by Dr. Barkley, to be present in the operating theatre during the planned Caesarean section. I was thrilled. I thanked Rosalee for being so considerate, and she apologized once again for not having been there during the birth of Logan.

We were led into an elegant private room reminiscent of a five-star hotel. There was a queen size bed with a beautiful blue and white striped comforter, dark blue curtains and dark mahogany side tables. There were at least four recliners scattered across the large living space. The only thing that appeared out of place was the standard issue clothing, which was folded neatly at the bottom of the bed.

As instructed by the nurse, I changed into the one-piece gown, open at the back. There was no way of making this look elegant, or even having it close in the back for that matter. I placed my clothes in the top drawer of the dresser located in the corner.

My parents bid us farewell as Rosalee, Cynthia and I were shuffled into a smaller room where my anesthesiologist of choice, Dr. James Cloudston, was waiting. While there were many anesthesiologists who were technically excellent at their chosen sport, James was excellent at just being human. I appreciated the way that he always spoke with every patient, no matter their make or model, and put them all at ease. He was one of only a few in his profession that my patients constantly mentioned during their postoperative visits.

As I had heard him do so many times before, with so many of my patients, he went over the epidural procedure in detail, including the significant risks and complications. He outlined alternative methods of pain control. I consented readily to the epidural and assumed the position—seated on the edge of the stretcher, feet elevated on a chair, knees bent up to embrace my ever-expanding abdomen and back arched towards the ten centimetre needle that would be inserted between my vertebrae. It couldn't be more perfect!

Two hours later, with a fresh and recurrent scar on my lower abdomen, I held Lucas in my arms for the very first time. I would be fortunate enough to remember everything this time. Logan was sitting in a recliner beside the head of the bed. My parents, Audrey, Rosalee and Cynthia rounded out those who were all present and accounted for in the room. For a fleeting moment, my old friend Silence was also present, but he was quickly replaced by the cries of a new infant and the joy of those around him.

"Well, that was certainly easier than last time," Cynthia commented, being the only adult in the room who had managed to be present at the birth of both my children.

"I agree!" I exclaimed. The description of the events was shorter and less complicated than it was with the first. I was eternally thankful for that!

33

The Single Mother and Silent Innuendos

Several weeks following the arrival of Lucas, I was sitting in the afternoon sunlight on my favorite couch placed strategically near the south facing window of our family room. My parents had left two days previously, and although not known for being loud and disruptive people, the house was decidedly quieter with them gone. Lucas was asleep on my lap, snoring softly, while two of three cats lay resting quietly at his feet. Audrey and Logan were in the kitchen making chocolate chip cookies from scratch—not one of my areas of expertise. The doorbell rang, and I looked up at Audrey as she exited the kitchen and adjoining family room towards the front foyer. I could not see the front door from where I was seated, and I was not expecting anyone at 2:30 in the afternoon. I could not hear much except what sounded like the whispered conversation between Audrey and whomever was at the door. As I strained to hear, I thought it sounded like a male voice, somewhat familiar, but one I could not easily place.

I deftly pushed myself up and off the couch with my left arm, while Lucas remained asleep in the crook of my right arm. Logan was now heading for the front door as I rounded the corner behind him, slowly and precisely so as to not wake Lucas. There, standing beside Audrey who had closed the front door so as to keep out the heat of this warm July afternoon, was Lieutenant Steeves in full standard police uniform, including his weapon!

"Hello," he offered, extending his hand out towards Logan. "Who might you be?"

"Logan," replied my oldest son who seemed to stand up straighter in response, and whose attentions had been involuntarily seized by the gun the Lieutenant had holstered on his right hip.

Lieutenant Steeves shifted his gaze to follow the path of where Logan was focused. His demeanor seemed to suggest that he was embarrassed that he had forgotten to remove his weapon before entering a civilian home. He shifted slightly such that his gun was only somewhat further away from Logan.

"Lieutenant Steeves, Randy," he responded while shaking Logan's hand. Lieutenant Steeves focused his attention on me as he educated all of us, including myself, on his first name. "I am a friend of your mommy's. Would it be all right if I were to speak with her alone for a few minutes?"

As usual, Logan beamed as he was recognized as being important enough that someone needed to seek his approval in order to speak with his mother. "Sure! I am cooking cookies if you need any. Cookies are Mommy's favorite!"

"Good to know," Lieutenant Steeves replied, smiling and turning his attention towards me. "Is there a place we could speak?"

"Sure, what is this about?"

"I just wanted to bring you up to date about your file, which we will be closing later today."

"This way." I motioned him toward the living room at the north end of the house with my left hand. Lucas had not budged.

At the far end of the room, in front of the north facing window, sat two chairs with a small table in between. *That looks safe,* I thought, as I moved toward the window. I wondered what particular type of safety I was concerned about given that I was in the presence of a fully qualified police officer who was carrying a gun! I thought it best if we kept this meeting short and to the point. I was not as gracious as my oldest son and chose not to offer any food or drink. That might lead Lieutenant Steeves to think that this was more of a social visit than a professional one. I was wondering why this thought was even crossing my mind. I motioned for him to sit in the seat across from me on the other side of the intervening table.

"What would you like me to know?" I asked. It all felt very awkward, given the circumstances of our last meeting. I did not know exactly where to divert my eyes, and I wasn't sure what colour my face was, although it felt like it was flushed. Once again, my heart rate was up, and I was somewhat flustered. My thoughts were centred on getting this guy out of here before Lucas woke up and wanted to breastfeed. I also did not want to get into discussions about where my son's father was, what he did, or otherwise.

He took my lead and appeared to be all business in his

approach. "As you are aware, Martin is currently residing in British Columbia in a drug rehabilitation program. We were able to recover all the remaining missing prescriptions from your restricted prescription pad. Martin has confessed to acting alone, without the guidance or involvement of yourself or your previous nanny, Melissa," he said as he looked up and directly into my eyes. "The case is closed against you. The department wishes to thank you for your assistance in this very important matter."

"You are welcome," I replied, keeping his gaze. "I appreciate all that you have done for us. Is there anything else?"

"Um ... No ... No ... that's pretty much it. I just thought I would stop by and let you know as it saves you a trip down to the station." He turned his gaze towards the floor.

"Thank you," I replied glancing down at Lucas who was still resting comfortably. "Pretty much have my hands full here!"

"I can see that! Your nanny was telling me that the baby is just several weeks old. Congratulations! I don't think that we even knew that you were pregnant when we visited you last December."

"Pregnant and sick as a dog! I thought I might puke on someone during that conversation!" As soon as it was said, I regretted it. Pregnant and sick as a dog? That was definitely too much information.

Lieutenant Steeves was not deterred or embarrassed by what I had just said. It seemed as if he accepted it as more of an invitation for casual conversation.

"That would not have been good! It is very difficult to get puke out of standard issues."

We both laughed, in a muted fashion, recognizing that

The Single Mother and Silent Innuendos

there was an infant precariously perched in my arms; an infant who could awaken at any instant.

"I would be up to the offer for chocolate chip cookies," he said.

I was silent for a moment. I was contemplating stepping over the threshold from a professional to a somewhat less professional relationship with Lieutenant Steeves. I was unsure how I was going to balance this. I was not wanting to appear like I was being standoffish and rude as a host.

The silence had obviously gone on too long as Lieutenant Steeves was starting to get up. "I appreciate your time. Perhaps it is best if I get going."

"No, that is all right. Logan and Audrey are known for making some of the best chocolate chip cookies this side of the Canadian Rockies." Certainly, there would be no harm in a few cookies, or so I thought.

We got up and made our way towards the kitchen. As we exited the narrow doorway from the living room and into the adjoining hallway, he stepped back and allowed me to exit first. As I walked passed him, I could smell his cologne and feel the heat that was once again rising between the two of us. I thought that perhaps I was imagining it, or that maybe he was feeling it too. I did not know exactly what to think, although I knew what I wanted to do. Luckily, that was not possible with an infant resting in my arms.

We entered the kitchen, and I noticed that Logan and Audrey had been hard at work. The circular table at the far end of the kitchen was set with four places, each accompanied by a nametag in Logan's four-year-old awkward handwriting. The cards read Logan, Audrey, Mommy and Randy. Lieutenant Steeves walked directly over to the table and started pouring milk into each of the four glasses that accompanied each of the four designated seats. We all accepted our assigned positions.

The next hour passed very quickly. There was idle chatter about what it was like to be a police officer, that passed back and forth, mostly between Logan and Lieutenant Steeves. There were a great number of cookies consumed and a great amount of milk which was enjoyed between the four of us. Lucas woke up once, and Audrey asked if she might take him into the other room, where it was quieter, to feed him. He had been given about three bottles over the last two weeks, all by Audrey, and seemed very comfortable with whatever he was offered. She returned, having achieved great success, within about fifteen minutes. During that time, Logan, Lieutenant Steeves and myself spoke about what it means to be a police officer, and Logan was invited to come for a tour of the station. It was all very strange, yet all very perfect and comfortable.

As the time approached 4:30 p.m., I got up and advised Logan that we should let Lieutenant Steeves get back to work. Logan, Lucas and I walked Lieutenant Steeves to the door and bid him farewell. Lieutenant Steeves reached out his hand, once again, towards Logan. "It was great to meet you, Logan. I am looking forward to getting together again."

"Good-bye Randy," Logan beamed and ran off back to the kitchen.

"Thank you for stopping by, Lieutenant Steeves. It

is kind of the department to follow up, in person, when someone's case file is closed. It is probably much easier just to follow up by telephone."

As he stood there, seemingly not wanting to leave, he replied, "We usually do, however Detective Peters suggested that I might want to stop by in person. I wish you would call me Randy. I do not consider this purely a professional visit," he said, bringing his eyes back to lock with mine. "I want you to know that I know about your situation. Your nanny mentioned how consumed you are, what with being a single parent and all. I don't want you to think that I am the kind of man who will be easily deterred given that information."

I did not know what to say, or what to do, or where to go next. This was very much unlike me. I had always been a sucker for a man in a uniform, and here was one who appeared to have made a special trip to see me, and who was not frightened away by the story of my life. I was at once relieved, yet at the same time disgruntled, that it was the middle of the afternoon and that I was surrounded by my children and my nanny.

"Thank you," I simply said. "That is very kind of you." I could feel my heart rate escalating once again and the colour of my face rising from white to crimson. I lowered my eyes to look at Lucas.

"Would you mind if I called you, just you or all of you, whatever you like, sometime?" he inquired as he placed his right hand softly on my chin and turned my gaze towards his.

"Just me would be perfect," I heard myself utter as he removed his hand from my chin and inadvertently brushed his index finger against my lower lip in the process. I thought I heard myself gasp, although I wasn't quite certain given that it all seemed to be suddenly taking on a very surreal tone. From the slight hint of a grin that was developing on his face, I suspected that I had not imagined it.

"Good-bye, Dr. Victoria Jones," he said, smiling more broadly now.

"My friends call me Tori," I thought I heard myself say. "Good-bye Lieutenant Steeves, I mean Randy."

"I hope to see you soon, Tori."

I closed the door behind him.

What was I getting myself into? *He should really be more careful with his weapon,* I thought. *Which weapon?* I smiled to myself as I entered back into my fabulous world of motherhood.

34

Something Dangerous

After a brief discussion between me, myself and I, I texted Rosalee in the UK. She was seven hours ahead of us and deeply intrigued that I needed to speak with her, by phone, not by e-mail and not by text, somewhat urgently.

I am afraid I have done something dangerous! I need to speak with you urgently! Can you speak now?

It was going to be difficult for me to transition to Lieutenant Steeves' first name as it meant going from the formal to the informal, the professional to the familiar. This had not been a part of my modus operandi when it came to my social interactions with men, for a very long time. It was also not aligned with the tightly orchestrated script of how my life was supposed to unfold as a single mother by choice, not once, but now twice with the recent addition of Lucas to the mix.

It was midnight in the UK, and I was surprised to see her response flash up at the top of the screen.

I can speak now. Just getting the place unpacked. I will call you.

Rosalee also preferred to text in near complete sentences, and I would have it no other way. We were apart by distance, but close as friends, and I knew that she would set me straight. Lucas had just been fed and was being rocked in his swing. Audrey and Logan were cleaning the kitchen after a very successful afternoon cookie party.

I answered my phone on the first ring. "Hello, Rosalee! Thank you for calling."

"What is going on? Your text said that you have done something dangerous. You have intrigued me as you are generally someone who does not wander far from their designated life script. Have you or one of the children been injured?"

"No."

"Well then. Did you quit your job, change your hair colour or perhaps order food from a new and unknown restaurant?" she inquired jokingly.

"No! Nothing like that!"

"Well, do tell then!"

"Remember when I was telling you about the three police officers who showed up at my clinic near the end of December before the shit hit the fan with Melissa?"

"Yes. I remember that whole thing as being a very difficult time for you. I wish that you did not have to go through that. Has something else arisen out of that?"

"No ... Yes ... No..." I replied. "Not exactly."

"Well, what is it then? Please do not keep me in suspense. It seems as if everyone is safe. Am I right?"

"Physically safe."

"What does that mean?"

"Lieutenant Steeves, one of the officers from that fateful encounter, dropped by the house today. He wanted to let me know, in person, that Melissa's boyfriend, Martin, had confessed that neither Melissa nor myself had any part in the narcotics fiasco."

"That is great! You are out of the woods and can now get on with your life! Congratulations! I can see why you wanted to let me know right away. I don't see, however, how this relates to you doing something dangerous. Is there something I am missing?"

"The reason I wanted to speak with you has nothing to do with that. While Lieutenant Steeves was here, he suggested that he would like to get together again."

"But the case is now closed. What would be the ... Oh, did he ask you out?" she inquired gleefully.

"Yes, I think so. Not me exactly, but me and Logan and Lucas. I told him that it would just be me."

"Well! That is dangerous, at least it is dangerous for you!"

"What does that mean?"

"You know what that means. No one else I know would refer to this as having done something dangerous. You accepted an offer to get together with someone for ... for what ... for coffee?"

"I am a single mother with two children, one only a few weeks old! There is no way this can go any further. I need you to walk me through what I will say to Lieutenant Steeves when we meet in person. I need to make it perfectly clear that this can go no further. And yes, it will be for coffee only!"

"Why do you need me to walk you through this? If that is how you feel, simply tell him. Why do you need me? Why do you keep referring to him as Lieutenant Steeves? Certainly, if he asked you out, you must know his first name."

"His name is Randy. I need to be perfectly clear with him when I meet with him. I have a life plan, a very structured life plan, which I can't deviate from."

"Can't or won't? I know you have been through some crap, some very serious crap, with men in the past. Don't let that stop you from at least meeting and speaking with the guy. Hell, does he know your story?"

"I think so. He said that Audrey told him I was a single mother and of course he knows all about my run-in with the law and the whole fertility fiasco."

Rosalee started to laugh, "And he still asked you out? This guy must be very intrigued. How did he know where you lived?"

"That's the other thing. It is all very creepy. The guy drops by out of nowhere, spends a few hours eating cookies with my family, and now expects me to go out with him?"

"Let me get this straight—he spent a few hours eating cookies with you and you are questioning his motives. Hell, I don't think I would spend two hours eating cookies with you!"

"Are you going to help me or not?"

"Yes, however I think I will help you out by not being coerced into participating in your ludicrous plan. It is obvious he is interested in you, and it is obvious you are interested in him or you would not be asking me to rehearse what you are going to say to him. You are my best friend, and I love you, but you are on your own with this one. I suggest you try to just go with it!"

I did not know how to respond. Of course, she raised

some very good points, and I knew she was right. I had been through a lot of crap in my relationships with men, and I knew that this was clouding the issue. My main concern, however, was that I had never considered how to incorporate something such as this into my difficult work-life balance. She was right, I did have feelings for this man, and that was my main impetus for trying to get her to rehearse what I was going to say to him.

"Are you still there?" she ventured after several moments with Silence.

"Yes,"

"You know I have only your best interests at heart. Do you disagree with what I am saying?"

"No, I do not disagree with you. It would just be easier to forget the whole thing and retreat earlier rather than later."

"Easier, but far less interesting, I would think?"

"I am not sure I need more interesting things in my life right now!"

"That is ultimately for you to decide, however I would urge you to at least consider that this could be something beneficial for you."

"I wish you were here to help me through this. I am not sure that I am capable of working through this alone right now."

"You are not alone! You are as close as a phone call or a text away. You know that!"

"Yes, I know that. It would be great, however if you could just fly home and sit between Lieutenant Steeves and myself when we meet for coffee."

"His name is Randy and what would be the fun in that?"

"Again, not looking for more fun or more interesting things in my life right now. The guy would have to be—"

Rosalee cut me off. "Maybe you should be looking for more fun, Tori. Listen, it is late here, and I have to be at work early in the morning."

"Of course," I responded, looking at the time, which now read 5:45 p.m. "Thank you for everything and take care."

"You too, Tori! I am looking forward to hearing more in the near future."

"I bet you are!"

Maybe I would be lucky and Randy would not contact me. I hoped that would not be the case.

35
1+1+1 – Success!

It was almost a week later and no word from Randy. I was genuinely relieved, I think, because now my reasoning was not being confounded by me being hot, bothered, and with dreams of being ravaged on some deserted island. Now I was just hot and bothered. Logan, although not initially in direct competition with Lucas, seemed to be vying for more and more of my attention. Breastfeeding was becoming increasingly difficult, and Logan wanted to do more than just build newer and more exciting Lego creations. Don't get me wrong, Audrey was a godsend, however Logan was asking more and more from me. Audrey and I were spelling off, when we could, but both my sons wanted everything I could give—and then some.

The postpartum team stopped by every day to see, no ensure, that I was still breastfeeding. They were always pleasant, encouraging, and left with the same gentle reminder—it is only one feeding every three hours! As the door shut behind them, I would think to myself 'sure one feeding that lasts almost an hour with an almost four-year-old crawling all over me'. Audrey and I hid the illicit formula just prior to the team arriving on each successive day.

I should have known that things were not going to go well that day. It was approaching 37°C, almost 100°F, and Logan awoke not feeling well. It started with nausea and vomiting and quickly progressed to diarrhea. Not just regular diarrhea, but every twenty minutes 'My belly hurts. Please help me, Mommy. I think I am going to die' kind of diarrhea. The only saving grace was that no one else, including Lucas, seemed to be sick. Audrey was at the pharmacy getting Pedialyte and Gravol. We had agreed that she would take over the care of Lucas once she returned, while Logan and I retreated to live in the bathroom for as long as it might take.

By the time Audrey returned, the vomiting seemed to have stopped. Logan was able to get about six ounces of Pedialyte into him before he ran to the washroom again. He didn't have far to run as we had set up a little picnic site right outside the bathroom. Still, he just made it in time. I was sitting close to him and wishing that I could take his place; I would have given anything to take his place. This is when I happened to look over and see that the box of Gravol had spilled out of the pharmacy bag. I glanced at it just long enough that my subconscious brain registered 'suppository', which was written across the front in large blue letters. I turned my attention back to my very distressed oldest son who was asking for more Pedialyte and a cool facecloth.

I gave Logan more Pedialyte and had him lie on the cool tiles of the bathroom floor. I washed my hands, for the umpteenth time, and opened the box of Gravol. As I was thinking that the pills looked a bit off, the word 'suppository' flew directly out of my subconscious mind landing in the middle of my grey matter. Suppositories! Suppositories?

I called downstairs to Audrey and told her that she must have made some kind of mistake. I was unsure how I was supposed to successfully insert a suppository when it would surely have to fight against the torrential downpour of an ever-increasing stream of diarrhea in order to be successful.

Audrey appeared in the doorway and apologized for failing to mention the suppository thing. The pharmacist had said that this was the best way to ensure that Logan was going to get the medication. Her eyes settled on the pharmacy bag, and like a magician, she picked it up and extracted four pairs of rubber gloves which had previously gone unnoticed in this particular magic trick. She was good, damn good!

"Lie him down after poo. Wear gloves and put pill up bum."

"As simple as that?" I asked.

"That's what the man in the store told me."

The man in the store! I was about ready to ask her if this was just some guy off the street or whether it was the pharmacist who had told her this. Logan began to cry.

"Mommy, I have to go again!" he exclaimed.

I picked him up and place him on the toilet. There was not much action over the next few minutes, however he claimed he was done. I laid him down on the floor once again. I explained what I was going to do and thought about how sick he must be as he did not object at all. I took one of the suppositories and laid down facing him on the floor. I laid my right hand between his left cheek and the floor and I deftly inserted the suppository with my gloved left hand. Not bad! He did not even flinch. After about thirty seconds, the suppository shot out.

Logan looked at me. "Mommy, I don't feel better.

"I know, honey. Mommy needs to try again."

"All right," he offered without even cracking a smile. "Good luck."

I wondered whether I should use the same suppository again, seeing as how the five second rule was unlikely to apply here. I picked it up and looked it over and decided that it somehow just didn't feel right. There were eighteen suppositories in that stupid package, and my son deserved a shiny new one. I did set that one aside, however, as I was concerned we might make it all the way through the package and have to start at the beginning again.

I took the second suppository in my gloved left hand and assumed the position with my right hand between Logan's cheek and the tile floor. I deftly inserted the second suppository and thought about how many times, in the history of mankind, parents had been trapped in this same predicament. I left my left hand in the launching position for about five minutes before moving it. After about thirty seconds, the second suppository shot out.

Really! I thought. *Really!* I removed the glove from my left hand, washed my hands and picked up the Gravol box to read the directions. They were quite simple, really, and appropriately written in Grade 8 English. They instructed me to wear gloves, take a single suppository and insert per anus. My thoughts went to all the patients I had ever operated on who did not have an anus anymore. What were they supposed to do? "Never mind that," I said out loud to anyone who would listen. "You can't even figure out how to do this with someone who actually has an anus!" Luckily, I was one of those individuals who fiercely rose to the occasion when faced with something that could not be done. There was no way that a small suppository and my son's anus were going to get the best of me!

I picked up a third suppository, placed another glove on my left hand and reassumed the position. Logan looked at me and smiled. I did not think that it was lost on this small child, not yet four, that his mother was unable to accomplish this simple task.

"Third time lucky!" I exclaimed as I inserted the third suppository.

"Third time lucky," Logan softly repeated for encouragement.

I awoke sometime later to the soft sounds of Logan gently shaking me. My left hand was still in launch position and there was a large deposit of drool where my mouth had lain against the bathroom floor. My right hand was glued to Logan's cheek.

"Mommy, I feel better! I am starving. I can't move with your hand on my butt!"

"I am sorry, Logan," I announced, pulling my hand away. I noticed that Audrey was now standing at the door with Lucas in her arms. Her face held a look of concern and amusement. "Why don't you wash your hands, get dressed and Audrey will make you some toast with butter?"

"Sounds great! I starving!"

Logan got up and washed his hands. He placed his right hand in Audrey's left, her right arm housing small Lucas.

They all turned to exit the washroom.

"Good work, Mommy!" Logan exclaimed over his right shoulder as they left.

"Thanks!" I must be much better at this than most. I had only needed to use three of the four pairs of gloves to accomplish this mystifying feat! Now that was a true measure of success!

36
Tragic Past Lives

It had been almost three weeks since I had heard from Lieutenant Steeves. We were getting back into a normal, well at least a regular, routine. I was thankful for Audrey and the stability that she brought to our small family unit. I had only reverted to my 24-hour list on a few occasions.

Lucas was almost two months old and flourishing. I was no longer breastfeeding, and he didn't seem to mind. The postpartum team and I had parted acrimoniously when they took exception to my failure to extract myself from the upstairs bathroom for one of their daily visits just over two weeks ago. Logan had been exceptionally ill, and I had been learning the intricate steps involved in the insertion of rectal suppositories. Besides my success in mastering this complex maneuver, I had successfully managed to prevent the postpartum team from returning ever again! I had managed to kill two birds with three suppositories!

I had told Audrey that when Lucas was two months old, I was going to take one day a week to go into the office or address whatever else was on my plate. We agreed it would be Thursday. On Wednesday evening at about 5:30 p.m., with my emotions being a mixed bag between excitement, apprehension and doubt, my cell phone rang. I absently picked it up as I followed Logan to the washroom to brush his teeth.

"Hello, this is Dr. Victoria Jones."

"Tori, this is Randy, Randy Steeves."

"Hello, Lieutenant Steeves," I responded flatly, hoping that he would not miss the faint hint of anger in my voice. I had often wondered how I would respond if he were to call. As time wore on, my emotions had gone from excitement to confusion and now to anger. I reminded myself to stay calm.

"Please call me Randy."

"Hello, Randy. What can I do for you?"

"I was wondering if you could meet for coffee tomorrow. It has been a while since we last spoke, and I wanted to have the opportunity to explain myself."

"I am busy tomorrow. I am starting back to work and will be at the office all day."

"I will take only about half an hour."

"Is this not something that can be done over the telephone?" I asked.

"I would prefer not to, Tori."

There was something in his voice that was extremely sad and lost. I reminded myself that I had no idea why he had not called. Perhaps he just got busy, although I did not know how anyone could be any busier than I was. Perhaps something else had happened.

"There is a forest with walking trails behind the hospital. I could meet you by the front doors at about 1:00 p.m., and we could go from there. You say you need about half an hour? I will schedule you in for thirty minutes." Even though my whole afternoon was basically free, I wanted him to understand that this was not going to last for longer than half an hour at the most.

"I know where that is. I will see you at 1:00 p.m. sharp. Thank you."

"Good-bye, Lieutenant Steeves," I said flatly, and hung up.

Needless to say, I did not sleep well that night. I was again hot and bothered, and it wasn't the weather. My thoughts alternated between wondering what possible reason there could be for his failure to call sooner and what he was like in the sack. I was finding it increasingly more difficult to keep my mind off the latter. That infuriated me even more! Aside from the way that he filled out his uniform, he did not deserve the time that I was dedicating to imagining what it would be like to have my hands all over him! Every time I tried to reignite my anger, he would reappear, shirtless, from the back reaches of my mind. I wondered how much more difficult this was going to be in person. What had I done by agreeing to meet with him alone in the woods?

I arose at 6:30 a.m. and did twenty minutes on the elliptical machine—all that Dr. Barkley was allowing me. I had a shower and got dressed. I chose a long red wool dress with a black belt and leather boots. The dress contrasted well against my blonde hair and seemed to hide the fact that I had been very pregnant just a short time ago. I went out to the kitchen by 7:30 a.m. where Audrey was already standing by the sink.

She turned to me and said, "Don't worry. I take care of the boys. Don't worry."

"I won't worry." I had other things to worry about today.

I got into my car and took the familiar drive to the hospital, the last time being when I had my staples removed following my second C-section. It felt good, and I was looking forward to the day, aside from the apprehension that I felt surrounding my 1:00 p.m. appointment with destiny.

I let myself into my office and thought about how nothing much had changed in my brief absence. There were three large piles of paper arranged precisely on my desk. My assistant, Lori, had always put things into three piles. I had often wondered what would happen if I were away for an extended period of time. I supposed that I would have to purchase a stepladder.

I started working eagerly through the piles. When I looked up, I was shocked to find it was already 12:30 p.m. It was not often I was able to get this much work done.

I got up and went to the nearest washroom to freshen up. I only bumped into two people I knew on the way, and thus the whole process took only about fifteen minutes or so. I locked my office door as I had done so many times before and retraced the maze of hallways back to the front door that I had entered that very same morning. My heart was racing, and I was started to get hotter. "Calm down," I heard myself saying from somewhere off in the distance.

As I exited the front door and turned my head to the left, I gasped. Randy was standing not ten feet from me wearing civilian clothes and looking directly at me. I had forgotten that I had never seen him in anything except his uniform before, and I was not disappointed! Aside from the familiar blond hair and piercing blue eyes, he wore a navy blue, short sleeved t-shirt, which fit him like a glove. This carried down to a pair of exceptionally nice fitting Levi's with light brown Cabela hiking boots. His hair and eyes were exactly as I had remembered them—how could I forget?

As I got closer to him, I started to feel more awkward. There was a feeling of intimacy and yet a feeling of unfamiliarity and strangeness. I could sense that he was feeling the same way. For that reason, and to stop myself from reaching out to touch him in some way, I turned around and started walking in the other direction.

"This way. I only have a brief period of time."

"Right."

There was an awkward silence that ensued for about the next fifty metres as we entered into the forested area behind the hospital. There seemed to be no one around at this time of the day, during this time of the year. I was not sure that I would be thankful for that.

I saw a bench directly ahead of us; a bench that I had sat upon numerous times. It faced a small pond, and it was presently unoccupied. Without turning around, I asked, "Is this all right?"

"Perfect."

We sat down on the bench with about three feet of space between us. He looked up, and sensing that I would probably not run away, moved only slightly closer.

"So," I started, "what did you need to speak with me about?" As I said this, I thought that I should probably not have almost sprinted during our journey out here. I did not want to appear flustered or out of control, however I was almost out of breath following our brief jaunt.

I looked straight forward into the pond as I silently waited for my breath to return. I wanted to look over at him, however I was afraid of what that might lead to.

"Can you look at me, Tori?"

"I most certainly can. I have that ability." What kind of dumbass remark was that? I turned my gaze toward him and my heart jumped a little.

"I wanted to start by apologizing for coming on a little too strong last time we were together. In thinking about it afterwards, I reminded myself that you had a very young baby to care for. I think that is one of the reasons it took me so long to call. I was embarrassed." I had to give him that. Of all the men I knew, he was probably one of the best at maintaining his gaze when the conversation got heated. He must have had a good mother.

"One of the reasons?"

"You caught that," he muttered softly, as if he were wishing I had not been listening so intently. He did not seem to know what to say, and therefore turned his gaze down toward his hands, which were fidgeting as they sat in his lap. I guess I must have overestimated him.

He looked back up at me and said, "I am going to be perfectly honest with you."

Great, I have not overestimated him. Crap!

"Recognize that I am not trying to buy your sympathy with what I am going to tell you. I offer it only as a way of explanation."

"Go ahead."

"I have known Lieutenant Blackstone for a long time, and Detective Peters even longer. During that time, I have dated no one, no one seriously, in a long time!"

"What does this have to do with me?"

"I am getting to that. It has been such a long time now. Aside from a few lifers on the force who have known me forever, no one knows my story."

I was intrigued and glanced up at him from where my eyes had come to rest on the pond. He looked as if he were going to cry and at the same time he looked almost relieved that he was going to be getting something, I am not sure what, off his chest. He was slouched over now and looked totally vulnerable. I wanted so badly to reach out to him.

"Go on," I said, turning slightly more towards him.

"I have not dated anyone for over ten years," he continued, "not seriously anyways. There were a few dates here and there, but no one who sparked my interest in the least. Mostly, very superficial women, if you know what I mean. They seemed to be enamored only by the uniform."

Perhaps much like I am. I looked at his upper arms as they arose out of his t-shirt and decided that I liked this uniform as well.

"When we came to visit you that day at the hospital, it started off as just another normal day in a long stream of normal days. Nancy, Lieutenant Blackstone; Rick, Detective Peters, and I have worked together forever. We operate like a well-oiled machine. However, as soon as I rounded the corner into your office that day, I could sense there was something different about you. I was not expecting it. All I knew about you, besides the fact that you are a surgeon, was the information we were given on the previous fertility clinic escapade. Even though I knew you were a physician, a surgeon, I expected you to be a flake." He looked right at me, shrugged his muscled shoulders and said, "I'm sorry for that!"

"And?"

"And you proved me wrong, very wrong," he said, shaking his head. "It was in the way you answered every question directly and sincerely, and how you were willing to help us do the right thing. Not a lot of people like that."

"Thank you," I considered it a great compliment.

"I noticed it, Nancy noticed it, and even Rick noticed it. I know he is the Detective, but Rick is generally the last one to notice things."

"What did they notice?"

"That I was flustered and had a hard time getting the words out. Before we meet with anyone, we always talk about who is going to stand where, who is going to lead the conversation and even how we are going to exit. We like to appear professional and to put forward a united front. Where it really became apparent was when we got set to leave, and I stepped back towards you rather than exiting first."

"I remember."

"That shocked even me! The three of us have worked together for a long time, and we ... I... have never gotten it wrong before. Even before we left the hospital, the two of them were on me with questions like 'Do you know her?', 'What was that all about?', and even my favorite 'Can we get you two a room?'"

He moved slightly more towards me. I could sense we were nearing the half hour mark, but I wanted to hear more. I wanted to hear all of it. I was definitely in danger!

"I brushed them off, at first, and for only a few days.

I couldn't stop thinking about you, and I didn't know what to do about it. They noticed it, especially Rick. He reminded me that nothing could happen during the time we were working the case. They warned me about even tempting myself by looking up your number or your address. I worked the case hard. I was convinced that you had nothing to do with it, but Martin would say nothing. Eventually, when it became apparent that Melissa was going to go down, he confessed to the whole thing and absolved the two of you of any wrongdoing."

"Wow."

Randy smiled slightly. I could tell there was still something bothering him.

"When we knew the case would be closed, Rick suggested that he make a special request to the department to tell you in person. I didn't think they would go for it, hell Rick didn't think they would go for it, but they did!"

"I had mixed feelings about the whole thing and wanted Rick and Nancy to accompany me. They both adamantly refused. They told me that this was for me to figure out on my own." This was beginning to sound a lot like the late-night conversation that Rosalee and I had had some several weeks earlier when Randy had first visited my home.

He looked like a naïve little boy as he continued with his story. I began to wonder how old he really was. Certainly, he must be younger, perhaps significantly younger, than my more than forty years.

"Before I visited your house that day I had myself convinced that I would tell you we had closed the case and that would be that—end of discussion. I had myself convinced that what I felt in your office was not real—that it was just the place and the time.

"Your nanny opened the door. When I asked if you were at home and if I might speak with you, she replied that you had just had a baby, that you were a single mother, and that I should not disturb you for too long. I think she only agreed to let me in because I was in uniform. That was when Logan rounded the corner, followed closely by you and Lucas. I knew I was not going to make it out of there unscathed."

I had not noticed, but during the course of our conversation we had shifted and were now sitting directly beside each other. "What do you mean by that?"

"As soon as your nanny told me about Lucas, I surmised that you must have been pregnant when we first attempted to interrogate you in your office last December. I was turning to leave, but Audrey had already closed the door behind me. That was when you rounded the corner."

He looked directly at me with a kind of deep sadness that I did not understand. Again, he looked as if he wanted to cry. I put my hand on his knee, and asked, "Are you all right?"

At first his whole body seemed to tense, and I thought he was going to take my hand, pick it up and place it back in my own lap while explaining that I was being inappropriate. Almost as quickly as he tensed, he seemed to completely relax, and then he started to cry. There were not just a few tears; I mean he really started to cry. He brought his hands up to his face and tried to console himself. I didn't quite know how to react as it seemed out of context with the whole discussion.

"I'm sorry," he finally said.

"It's all right. We don't have to do this now."

"What about the half hour rule?"

"Screw the half hour rule!" I exclaimed. God, was I ever in deep trouble!

"I have to do this now, or I don't know that I will ever be able to. I promised Rick that I needed to tell you today as I think it partly explains why I haven't called you. You see, I haven't dated anyone in ten years for a reason. The last woman I loved, the only woman I have ever loved, was killed in the line of duty when she was three months pregnant with our first child."

My hand was still resting on his knee, I think. I stared at him in disbelief. He was no longer crying, and in fact he seemed to be completely relaxed.

"I knew that if I did not turn around and leave that day, knowing that you had been pregnant when we first met, there would be no turning back for me. That day was one of the best days that I have had for a long time. Don't get me wrong, I love spending every waking moment of my time with Nancy and Rick," he said while rolling his eyes, "It just felt like home."

"When I got back to the precinct, I told Rick and Nancy that it had all gone according to plan. I told them that I had let you know that the case was closed and that I had thanked you for your assistance. I threw the file across my desk towards Rick. He just smiled and muttered five innocent words in my direction."

"Which were ...?"

"What took you so long? What took you so long? Hell, they didn't even have to interrogate me. It just all came spilling out—every perfect detail about that afternoon. I told them I was in danger, and they wouldn't even agree to protect me from you. I can't believe I am telling you all this."

I started to laugh uncontrollably.

"I am not sure what is so funny about this," he said.

"I don't know why I am telling you this either, but at the same time you were asking them to protect you from me, I was on the phone with my best friend informing her that she needed to protect me from you. Heck, it was even midnight in the UK where she lives!"

We both started to laugh.

"I didn't come here today expecting anything. I just needed to get everything off my chest. I don't know what will happen, all I know is that I have feelings for you. If this goes anywhere, you will have to be careful with me."

He leaned over towards me, took my face between his hands, and kissed me. At that moment, I didn't remember caring about much of anything except the fact that it was exactly as I imagined it would be. I could feel his tongue yearning for the inside of my mouth as if it had been waiting for that moment for an eternity. I couldn't say how long it lasted, all I know is that it was not long enough, by far.

"I can be careful with you," I finally gasped as we both came up for air. "Can you explain what you mean by that?"

"Screw it," he said, leaning over to kiss me again.

37
Taking it Slow

Randy and I had agreed to take it slow, and I had asked that we leave my kids out of it, at least for now. I had told him my story, most of which he had pretty much guessed, having already known about the 'fertility fiasco', as we had come to refer to it.

We were not seeing each other more than once or twice a week, mostly on account of his schedule! He was working some type of large narcotics scandal with Nancy and Rick, but he could tell me little else. We had been out once, for dinner, with Nancy, her husband James, and Rick. Nancy commented that it was nice to finally have one of them hooked up with somebody. I explained to everyone that we were taking it slow. I often wondered what taking it slow really meant. It wasn't like we were back in high school, so I assumed we weren't going to be taking it *that* slow.

As a single parent, my main concern was keeping this from Lucas, and especially Logan, until I was certain of what was going on. I often wondered how people navigated this difficult situation, especially when there were multiple adult parties involved. I was thankful there were children on just one side of the equation.

I was getting ready for the theatre that evening. We were going out with Nancy, James and Rick. I had been looking forward to this all week. We were seeing the Broadway production of Les Misérables and then taking in a late dinner. I had already explained to Logan that I would not be home until after he was asleep, and Audrey had instructed me to have a great time. I had not told Audrey what was happening with Randy as I was afraid she would let it slip.

I had bought a new dress, shoes, and purse for the occasion. The dress was black, low-cut and tight fitting. It had a gold belt at the waist and fell just below my knees. I topped it off with a thick gold chain and matching diamond stud earrings. I had made a concerted effort to get back into shape after Lucas was born, and it showed.

Logan looked up as I entered the family room. He came over to me, gave me a big hug and said, "Mommy, you look so beautiful!"

I was meeting Randy at his place, about a twenty-minute drive from my house. I was nervous on the way over, mostly because it was a formal event with his closest friends. "You have no reason to be anxious," I kept telling myself, but it wasn't working.

Randy opened the door seconds after I knocked. He was wearing a black polyester-wool blend suit with a dark grey silk shirt, a blue tie and black dress shoes. His eyes were stunning against the backdrop of the ice blue tie. I couldn't seem to take my eyes off of him. He invited me in for a drink and asked if he could take my coat.

"Sure," I said, slowly undoing first the belt and then the buttons of my shin length red wool coat with a Guess

Envelope collar.

"You are so beautiful, so sexy," he said, "It's hard to imagine that you are the mother of two kids under five *and* a full-time surgeon." I knew he had added that last part as an attempt to seduce me. He could not seem to take his eyes off of me. It was a look that I had not seen in him previously, almost a hunger.

"Come here," he said, enveloping me in his arms and drawing me closer. "I want to take you all in."

He started to kiss me softly, at first, and then with an urgency that I had not felt before. "You look so beautiful."

"You already said that," I laughed.

"I thought that it needed to be said more than once. "Hell, it deserves to be said multiple times, you look so beautiful!"

"You clean up pretty well yourself!"

"Thanks! Can I get you something to drink?"

"I would like some white wine. Remember that I am not driving for a few hours." I followed along behind him thinking about how great he looked, how great he felt, and how great he smelled.

A few minutes later, I had downed my wine. As Randy helped me on with my coat, he kissed the back of my neck. I was feeling a bit tipsy, and a shiver ran through my body. I turned to face him, grabbed his tie with both of my hands, looked directly into his eyes, and said, "You know, when you asked me if I wanted something to drink, I was thinking that the only thing that I would like to drink is you."

He didn't look shocked at all—more amused and intrigued. He took me into his arms and kissed me again, this time with even more urgency than before. I could feel him getting hard against my lower body. He moaned again. "Man, you are making this difficult, Tori."

"Making what difficult? I thought I was making it hard!"

"We have to get going or we are going to be late," he said as he ripped his eyes away from my intense gaze.

I think we were both relieved that we had to be somewhere else, at least I know I was. I knew that he wanted to take it slow, that he needed me to go easy on him, and I was trying my best. He looked frustrated, but happy, and commented that he had been waiting for years for Les Misérables to finally come to Calgary.

"You are going to love it! I have seen it three times, and each time it gets better and better."

"I am really looking forward to seeing it with you!"

We arrived at the theatre in time to catch a drink with everyone. Rick commented that I looked gorgeous, and Randy lamented that he had not used that word first. We made our way toward our seats just as the lights dimmed for the first act.

Randy placed his hand in mine as the opening number began, and the curtain rose. He was looking directly at me, rather than the stage. I looked at him, and we both smiled.

About ten minutes into the first act, Randy looked over at me, leaned close and said, "Why are we taking this so slowly? I know you are concerned about me seeing Logan and Lucas again, but we are both adults. I want you so badly." He brought both our hands into his lap, and I could feel that he was hard again.

I turned and whispered in his ear, "I was under the impression that you were the one who wanted to move slowly! It may be against the law, but hell I would do you right here, right now, if you wanted me to."

He didn't flinch. He took his cell phone out of his pocket and texted someone. He grabbed me by the hand and excused himself repeatedly as we crawled over about ten people, in the dark, and made our way toward the exit. We picked up our coats and again he kissed the back of my neck, this time almost biting it. We made our way to the parking lot without saying a word. We found his car, he opened the door for me and then let himself in.

"Are you sure about this?" he asked.

"Yes! We are not children, or teenagers, or even young adults. We are middle-aged adults who both know what we want. I know this will probably complicate things, but I am already in over my head. Whether we sleep with each other or not will not change things for me. I think, though, that you have to be clear that you are ready."

He started his truck, a new 2008 black Dodge Ram, and navigated the fifteen kilometres home from the theatre in about twenty minutes. He was cheerful and appeared relieved. I asked him whom he had texted.

"I texted Rick to let him know you had child care issues and that we had to leave."

"Do you think he will buy it?"

"I don't care if he buys it, I just didn't want them to worry."

We entered into the front foyer of Randy's house. He took my coat and my purse and laid them gently across the chair in the front hallway.

"I want you so badly," he said, "I have from the first time I met you."

"Really, the first time you met me?"

"Yes, that first time I met you in your clinic! I could have stayed and interrogated you all day!"

"Well, you are free to interrogate me now!"

He didn't need any more invitation than that. His kiss was less urgent now, perhaps because it knew it was going to get him to where he needed to go. He moved down toward the cleavage of my dress and moaned. He grabbed my hand, and we made our way down the hall to what I assumed was going to be his bedroom. He did not turn on the lights, rather he flicked a switch near the door and the fireplace roared to life.

He led me over to the bed. "I want you. I have wanted to be inside of you so desperately for so long," He removed his suit jacket and let it fall to the floor.

"I am here for the taking," I whispered in his ear. This made him moan again.

I was glad to see he was in no hurry. He laid me on the bed and undid the belt that surrounded my waist. He continued to move between kissing me on the lips, on the neck and then down towards my upper chest.

"Is everything all right?" I asked.

"Are you sure this is what you want, I mean really want?"

I reached up and brought him down on the bed beside me. I reached my left hand down and could feel how hard he was. He moaned when I touched him. I positioned myself over top of him and gently swept the fingers of my left hand inside the front of his pants. I could feel his rigid cock reaching up to meet me in anticipation.

"Oh my god," he muttered.

I could feel him tense under me. I laid my head beside his left ear, and exhaled as I softly uttered, "I know my

Taking it Slow

male anatomy very well."

He moaned again as I slowly undid his pants. I was not disappointed. His cock was so hard, and so large, and so willing. Everything about him seemed rigid. He helped me unbutton his shirt, and I marveled as he freed first one arm and then the other. I threw his shirt on the floor and gasped as I looked down at him in the moonlight.

"You are so incredible!" I said, "And so hard!"

He pulled me close again and kissed me. He was back to being more urgent now. He was completely naked, and I was still nearly fully clothed. I loved the sense of power it gave me.

"I want you," he moaned.

"Not yet," I whispered in his ear.

"What do you want me to do?" he moaned, barely able to get the words out. "Anything."

"I want you to lie there and just enjoy it." He could see me in the moonlight above him. I reached down and noticed that he was dripping wet. I took what was being offered between the thumb and index finger of my right hand and moved my hand towards my mouth. I made sure that he was watching me. I leaned down and whispered, "You taste so good!"

His back arched, and he moaned again. I came down near his left ear and said, "I give good head!"

This made him wild. He flipped me over and unzipped my dress, which fell to the floor. He removed my bra and nylons and laid me naked on the bed. He looked down at me and smiled. "You are so beautiful!"

I reached up and flipped him onto his back. He did not seem surprised. He pushed my head down towards his hardened shaft, which was now throbbing in anticipation. I grabbed his hardness with my right hand and took the top of his penis into my mouth. With my left hand, I gently stroked the area between the back of his scrotum and his anus.

All I could hear as I took him all in was a constant moan and my name being repeated over and over again. "Tori, Tori, Tori, Oh my god!"

When he was close to climax, I removed my mouth and moved back up to kiss him. "I want you," I said, "Now!"

He flipped me over and climbed on top of me. He entered me with such force I thought that I might rip apart. He was so forceful as he thrust himself in and out of me. I was so wet. I reached up and placed my hands on his biceps, the part of him that I had first noticed those many months ago in my office. He slowed down and muttered that he didn't want to come yet; that he didn't want it to end. He was bathed in sweat, which was falling from him onto me with every thrust. He was kissing my face, first my eyes, then my forehead, then my nose and back to my mouth.

"Tori?"

"Yes," I gasped.

"I can't hold out much longer."

"That's okay. Neither can I," I moaned as my back arched, and I started to shake. I could feel him tense and moan again, this time from somewhere deep inside. He called my name one more time and then I could physically feel him coming inside of me. We had both worked hard at first to resist this and now to make it happen. I thought we had been more than successful on the second count.

Taking it Slow

I must have fallen asleep because sometime later I was awakened by Randy whispering in my ear. "How are you doing?"

"Great! You?"

"More than great!" he exclaimed. "I must say, that was better than I expected. I have never made love to someone who is a surgeon before." We both laughed.

He leaned over me and whispered, "I am getting hard again."

I reached down with both my hands to confirm that this was indeed the case, and again he moaned.

"I never could have imagined how good this was going to be," he said. "Do you have to get home?"

"I am all right. Audrey is with the kids."

"That's exactly the answer I was looking for." He reached down and grabbed my hands in his and brought them up between us. He looked at them intently for a moment and said, "You do have talented hands, very talented hands." He grasped my hands tighter and started kissing them. He looked at me and sighed, "Thank God for talented hands!"

"Thank you!"

"That was not exactly how I imagined it would go. I wanted it to be slower, less intense and more focused on what you need. That seemed a little too quick and too focused on me."

I could not believe what I was hearing! Out of all the men in the world, how had I been lucky enough to find this one? He leaned over and asked if I wanted to go back to sleep. He knew that tomorrow was going to be a busy day for me and the boys. He wanted to make sure that I got my beauty rest.

"So, you think I need my beauty rest?" I raised my eyebrows at him.

"Not at all! Just checking!"

Randy pulled the covers up around both of us. It felt good to just lie there in his warm, muscular arms. He asked me if I was comfortable, and I replied yes. I was lying on my back, on the right side of his king-sized bed, and he was lying with his right side down, his head propped up on his right arm, directly beside me. He pulled the sheets down to my navel and just stared.

"Your breasts are incredible. They are so soft and perfectly round."

"Thank you."

He was moving the fingers of his left hand slowly around my chest. As he neared each nipple in turn, he stopped and seemed to hover and make tiny circles with his index finger that were just large enough to encircle and tease the nipple itself.

He continued back and forth for what seemed like a very pleasant eternity. It was both soothing and arousing at once, and I seemed to float in and out of consciousness. After a period of time, his movements became less tentative and more demanding. I could feel the moisture rising between my legs. I moaned.

He leaned over and took my eagerly awaiting left nipple into his mouth. My left breast rose to meet him. His tongue moved slowly, encircling the small mound of flesh just as his fingers had done a few minutes earlier. His teeth softly teased the area where his tongue had just been. He was still encircling my right nipple with his left hand.

He pushed himself up on all fours over me. He repositioned his mouth over my right nipple, which rose toward him. His left hand was now searching between my legs, and it came to rest on my clitoris. It was obvious that he knew what he was doing with little instruction from me. He gently and repetitively, but insistently, worked me between the thumb and index finger of his left hand. He brought his mouth up next to my right ear and whispered, "I can give as good as I get!" I trembled with anticipation.

He moved down and replaced his left hand with his mouth. He was warm and quickly working his tongue in short flicks between my legs. His hands were at once deftly navigating the depths of my vagina and the area extending back toward my anus. I couldn't discern what was tongue, fingers, mouth or teeth, nor did I care.

I reached down and grabbed his wrists with my hands. I pulled him up towards me and met his warm mouth with my own. I could taste him and me, both of us at the same time. He grabbed my wrists and raised my arms above my head.

He began to enter me, but only partly and slowly. I begged him to enter me completely, but he refused. He seemed to be tempting me with his hardened weapon, and I was becoming more and more excited in anticipation of what I knew was coming next.

"Please! Please!" I begged, breaking my mouth free from his insistent kisses for only several seconds. This seemed to catch him off guard. I managed to move slightly down, forcing him inside of me, only slightly further, but enough. He finally gave in, not because he wanted to, but because he needed to. He thrust himself deep inside me.

He did not seem as desperate as he had previously. He stayed deep inside me for what seemed like an eternity, and then he slowly began to work me toward climax. He was slow and precise, each thrust only slightly more intense than the last. Every third or fourth cycle seemed longer, and it was at this time that he would bring his mouth up to my left ear and whisper, "I am working hard for you, baby! Tell me I'm working hard enough for you, baby."

Before I had time to answer, his mouth was back on mine, his tongue longingly searching within my mouth. He was becoming more impatient now. He pushed harder against me and more forcefully pinned my arms against the bed above me. He was working hard, very hard! I pushed equally hard against him, but to no avail.

From somewhere deep inside I could feel the sensation beginning to rise. It was more powerful than before, rising slowly at first toward the surface. I could feel every thrust, however it seemed to be just outside of my zone of conscious recognition.

I was brought back to reality by the sound of Randy whispering in my ear, "That's it, Tori, come with me!" I could feel my body respond to his insistent demands. The waves were more powerful than before, and they seemed to go on forever. I opened my eyes for only a second to see Randy on top of me in the similar throes of ecstasy.

The waves began to dissipate, however before I could regain my composure they were washing over me once again. My body arched toward Randy, and I could feel my entire body trembling. I could sense that Randy was watching me, but I could not respond. My mouth was dry, and my body ached. It was almost the best place that I had ever been.

The final crescendo was intense. I could hear myself scream out imperceptibly, with an almost guttural plea for resolution. I was unable to stop myself. "Oh my God, Oh my God", I repeated over and over. "Oh my God, Oh my God."

I could feel my body collapse in exhaustion. I was unable to respond as Randy collapsed on top of me and began to softly kiss the left side of my cheek, which was wet from the sweat of two bodies that had become one. I just wanted to drift into sleep.

Sometime later, I awoke to the soft sound of Randy snoring. I forgot where I was at first, confused by my new surroundings. I glanced over at the clock as I rose to consciousness. It read 3:12 a.m. As I began to drift back to sleep, I remembered that this was not where I needed to be. Like every other single mother, my few moments of respite were quickly overtaken by the need to care for my young children.

I shook Randy somewhat more than gently. "Randy, I have to go!"

"Please stay, Tori. I don't want you to leave."

"You know that I have to go."

He rolled over onto his back. "I will miss you before you are even gone."

I got up and moved quickly in the light of the warm fireplace. I dressed, kissed Randy softly on the lips and made my way towards the front door. It was cold as I escaped into the early morning air. It was sharp and sweet all at the same time. I let myself into my vehicle and enjoyed my time with Silence as I made my way back across the familiar city to a life that was urging me back to where I needed to be.

I knew where my home lay, where my heart lay, I thought as I entered through the garage. While happy for the superficial diversion that Randy presented, I knew that this was where I belonged.

38
Silence and Separation

Several weeks later, Logan and I were playing Lego on the family room floor. Logan's curly blond hair fell almost to his shoulders. He wore the same blue sweatpants, red shirt and black sneakers that he had worn for the last several days. Lucas lay sleeping in the sun on the floor beside me. I had dressed him in a dark blue onesie, which seemed to almost shine as the rays of sunlight reflected off his small chest and belly.

To deal with overcrowding in the Lego prison system, we were adding a third floor to the penitentiary. This had come to be a Saturday afternoon ritual for the three of us. Logan was engrossed in what he was doing. Little by little, brick by brick, we continued to build into the later hours of the afternoon. The third floor was my favorite color, purple, which contrasted with the black décor of the first and second floors.

As the clock approached 5:00 p.m., I could hear Lucas beginning to rouse. I laid my right hand on his chest and belly and let it rise and fall gently with his breathing. He was warm, and I noticed a small smile on his sleeping face. Could anything be more perfect?

We were going out for dinner with a friend, Samantha Haines, whom I had not seen for some time. Her children were about the same age as mine, two boys, and we were going to hang out at our local Boston Pizza. I was to return to work in just two days, and I was trying to touch base with as many friends, acquaintances and family members as I could before that fateful day. Of course, I had been in and out of the office during my maternity leave, just as I had been when Logan was born, however my mind was not as interested. Not only had my one-, three-, and five-year goals taken the back seat to these two small creatures, my 24-hour list had also often been tossed to the side. Not that I wasn't completing the desired elements on almost a daily basis, rather my mind was occupied by Logan and Lucas and Randy ...

I had seen Randy only twice since that glorious half night that we had spent together some two weeks earlier. Both times had been over coffee, and both times had seemed somewhat comfortable yet awkward. I didn't know where this was going, and I wasn't really interested in trying to define it. This was very much unlike me, and I didn't give a damn. Randy was as gracious as ever, and he had not mentioned seeing the children again, which I was thankful for. I did not know where I stood on this, as part of me yearned for him to be in our lives and part of me felt that there was nothing good that could come from including him at this time. I was not deeply committed to either idea and had decided that the tie breaker would be the passage of time. I had nothing but time.

I wondered how many single parents measured their romantic excursions in 'half nights' rather than full nights. There was a similar tension between being a good mother and a good surgeon that I felt between being a good mother and a good girlfriend—or whatever I was supposed to be. I dreaded my return to work as there was much more I was going to need to balance or integrate, and I was not looking forward to it. When I was away from Randy, I told myself that the right thing to do would be to end this now. And then I saw him ...

I got up and marveled at how far Logan and I had come over the course of the afternoon. We had completed the third floor and had begun the arduous task of moving prisoners into their new surroundings. I thought about how easy construction had been considering we did not have to put strong consideration into where the Lego figures would eat, sleep or even go to the washroom. I smiled and silently wished that my life was that easy. In my life there always had to be a time and a place for everything.

I reminded Logan that we would be leaving for Boston Pizza in about twenty minutes. He got up and started to gather up the stray Lego pieces from around the family room and even the kitchen. When he had finished, he knelt down and kissed Lucas on the cheek, looked up at me and smiled. He headed out towards the front hallway and off to his bedroom to start getting ready.

"Do you have to use the washroom?" I enquired over my shoulder in the direction of the hallway as I bent down to pick up Lucas and enveloped him with both of my arms.

"Oh yeah!" he exclaimed, almost as if this was a novel concept he had never thought of previously. He headed off towards the washroom and closed the door behind him.

I quickly dressed Lucas in his one-piece winter

costume, complete with feet and hands, and moved towards the adjoining garage door. I was buckling him into his car seat as Logan jumped in the other side and buckled himself in. *How independent for a four-year-old,* I thought, longing for the day when both my children would be able to buckle up. I made my way to the driver's seat and hoped that Lucas would remain slightly groggy during the five-minute ride to the restaurant, before I needed to feed him.

As we entered Boston Pizza, I saw Samantha and her two sons seated in a booth near the back of the restaurant. Like Lucas, her youngest son Kyle remained in his car seat and was resting on the floor next to his mother. Four-year-old Steven sat trapped on the inside, free to move around as long as he remained in his seat. The three of us arranged ourselves in mirror-like fashion across from the three of them. Logan and Steven were at once enthralled by a container of small tinker toys that Samantha had brought with her. Smart lady, smart mother!

I reached down to extract Lucas from his seat in preparation for his 6:00 p.m. feeding. As he settled in, I turned my full attention, whatever that means for a mother of small children, towards Samantha.

"How are things?" I inquired.

"Good, you?"

"All right. I am not sure if I'm coming or going most days, however we all seem to make it through to the next day, so I can't complain."

"I know what you mean! I don't know where the time goes, and I never seem to get anything done, but everyone seems healthy and happy."

"How is Stanley? What is he up to tonight?" Stanley was her devoted husband of seven years. Samantha and I had known each other long before he came into the picture, and given that I was seldom also coupled, he was someone I had not come to know well.

"Okay."

I looked across the table at her. Her dark brown hair hung straight to about five centimetres below her shoulders. She was wearing a lovely bright red cardigan, which accentuated the colour of her auburn hair and the sleekness of her high cheekbones. As my eyes rose up to meet hers, I noted a type of sadness or distance that I had not previously noticed.

"What's going on?" I asked.

She turned her attention towards Steven and Logan, ensuring that they were engrossed in their small cars. She then turned her head back towards me, and ensuring that I was looking directly at her, mouthed the words, 'We are separated'.

I started to laugh thinking that I must have misheard her, or rather misread her lips. I looked up to find her staring coldly in my direction. While the noise in the restaurant must have reflected the rowdy and boisterous clashes of the Saturday evening crowd, I heard none of it.

"What? When?"

"Two weeks ago. I don't want to talk about it right now. I am not sure what I was thinking when I thought I could speak with you about it on a Saturday evening, at Boston Pizza, with all the kids in tow." I could tell she was distressed, likely by the situation and likely by the inability to speak about it.

"Why don't we go back to my place? We can order in, open a bottle of wine and have more room and freedom to speak."

"I would love that! I was going to mention that, however did not want to intrude on you."

"No intrusion at all!"

We gathered up all our belongings, including the four children we owned between the two of us, and explained to our waitress that an emergency had arisen, and we had to leave. We proceeded in an unorderly fashion to the parking lot.

"I will meet you at my place in five minutes."

"I will be there."

As I got into my car, I felt an overwhelming sense of sadness. I knew how hard it had been, and was going to be, for me. I was thankful that I was not having to do this while engrossed in a demanding situation with a difficult ex-partner. I drove quietly out of the parking lot and towards my house. If Logan sensed that something was wrong, he was not saying anything. He was sitting quietly in the back seat, humming softly to himself, probably excited by the news that Steven was going to be coming over to our house to play.

I entered in through the garage and dialed Boston Pizza Delivery while still seated in my car. After reciting the all too familiar order for cheese pizza and boneless honey garlic wings, I retrieved Lucas from the back seat. Logan was already inside preparing for his very important dinner guest.

The doorbell rang just as I stepped into the house from the garage. Lucas and I made our way towards the front door, a mere ten steps, and opened it to invite Samantha and her two boys in. The early winter wind was very cold. I took their coats and deposited them in the front hall closet. We made our way to the family room, where the older boys excitedly started to envision a Lego city expansion.

I let Samantha know that I had ordered from BP. As I glanced over at Logan and Steven, I asked her if she would feel more comfortable sitting in the living room at the front of the house. She jumped at the opportunity. I instructed the boys that we would be just down the hallway if they needed anything. Neither one looked up or even acknowledged our presence. Samantha and I carried our two youngest sons down the hallway and into the dimly lit living room.

"What's going on?"

"I am not really sure. Stanley says he has been unhappy for a long time and that he doesn't know if it is the situation with the two young children, his job, or just him. He assures me that it is not me."

As I sat quietly thinking about what I might say next, given the pathetic excuses that were being offered by Stanley, I looked up at Samantha. The look of sadness remained deeply emblazoned across her dark blue eyes. There was no sense of anger or frustration that I could pick up on, just an overwhelming sense of tiredness and helplessness. I wondered how much was a reflection of her current circumstances, and how much was just motherhood. I wondered if I looked like that at times and shuddered at the thought.

"Are you doing all right?"

"I'm not even sure I know what that means right now. How would I know if I'm all right or not? I spend most of each day wondering if we're going to make it through to the next day and then I'm surprised when I awaken and find that we actually have."

"Who have you told?"

"No one."

I reflected back on a conversation with one of my surgical residents, Connie Lewiston. She had been deciding whether or not to leave her husband, surrounding an issue of motherhood, and she had not told anyone. I thought about how these situations were uncomfortable, for mothers and everyone involved. I wondered how many women were currently living this reality, surrounded by a planet of billions and billions of people, and finding that they had no one or only a few people to speak with. Silence was indeed a sad dancing partner during these troubled times.

"This must be very hard for you. Where is he staying?"

"We are both living at our place. I am on the main floor, and he is in the basement. It's the best we can do until we can figure out what to do with the finances and the children."

"Does that mean you are just talking about separating, or is it a done deal?"

"It is a done deal as far as I am concerned." This was the first time that I had seen a glint of anger in her eyes.

"It is very early. Perhaps ..."

"There is someone else! She is someone I don't know well. She is one of the other mothers from Steven's preschool class. Apparently, this has been going on for quite a

Silence and Separation

while and I am ... *THE ... LAST ... TO ... KNOW!*" Her intense gaze did not deviate from mine, and the glint of anger in her eyes became further entrenched.

"I am so sorry."

"Thank you. I know a lot of the mothers at the preschool. Only one had the decency to mention anything to me, even though people had been talking for months. I had been busy bringing Steven to class and picking him up when it was my turn. Meanwhile, parents all around me were aware and no one had the decency, until recently, to say a single thing!" Her voice was getting louder, and she was speaking faster now. I could feel the anger being directed at everyone, and no one, in particular.

"What are you going to do?"

"I am going to stay right where I am, and I am going to be the best damn mother I can be. As you know, I am taking a full year of maternity leave, and I have about six months left. I am not letting that ... asshole ... ruin the short time that I have with my children."

The doorbell rang, and two excited young boys ran down the hallway towards the front door from the direction of the family room. Nothing stood between my son and cheese pizza!

I opened the door, accepted the food, and handed it to Logan. He and Steven ran off towards the kitchen to start their feast. I paid by credit card, thanked the delivery person, and closed the front door. As I headed towards the kitchen, I turned back to see that Samantha remained seated in the living room, not having moved since before the doorbell rang. I yelled over my right shoulder, "Do you want something to eat, Samantha? Maybe a slice of pizza or a few wings?"

"No, thank you."

I helped the two older boys fill their plates with pizza and wings. Steven commented that he had never had honey garlic wings before and Logan told him that he didn't know what he had been missing. I laughed hearing this coming from the mouth of a four-year-old. I showed Steven how to eat a wing and then asked if they would be all right if I went back to the living room. They seemed excited that they would be taking care of themselves.

I returned to the living room to find Kyle and Samantha snuggling by the fireplace, which had now risen into action. How amazing this bond of motherhood is for most of us. She was softly singing something into his ear, and as I moved closer I thought I could hear the lyrics to *You are my Sunshine*.

You are my sunshine, my only sunshine;
You make me happy, when skies are grey.
You'll never know dear, how much I love you.
Please don't take my sunshine away.

As the last line drew to a close, Samantha sensed my presence and turned to face me. Tears were streaming down her face, and she began to tremble.

"What if he tries to take my children away?"

"That is not going to happen. You are a great mother!"

I looked over at Lucas, who was thankfully asleep in his vibrating chair in the corner. I thought about how I didn't even have to turn on the vibration anymore, about how he would almost instantaneously fall asleep when he was placed in it. I thought about how we all grow accustomed to things, and we never expect them to change. We never expect that we are going to be asked to deviate from our defined life path. I brought my chair closer to Samantha, and turning her face towards mine, I repeated, "You are a great mother!"

We sat there with Silence for some time as the air grew colder around us, and the tears subsided. I was thinking about whether being a great mother was in any way associated with children being allowed to remain with their mother. I didn't know the answer to this, and I was thankful that I was unlikely to ever be put in that situation. There were many hardships as a single mother by choice, however I was unlikely to ever have to think about someone pulling my children away from me.

Later that evening, when all was quiet and Silence showed her softer side, I thanked the universe that my life was as perfect as it was.

39
Too Many Men, So Little Time

I returned to work on a snowy day at the beginning of December. Audrey and I had been rehearsing for this eventuality over the last several months. Logan seemed to take it all in stride, being the independent young boy that he had always been. Lucas seemed to be adjusting well, and Audrey was stepping up to the plate. I, on the other hand, was a wreck. Returning to work this second time after maternity leave was far more difficult than the first time; far more difficult than I could have ever imagined. It was the first time that I had ever thought, for more than just a fleeting instance, that motherhood was more difficult than a surgical residency. I tried repeatedly to push that thought from my mind.

I was happy to be back at work, don't get me wrong. Being a surgeon was a big part of my identity, an important part of who I was at my core. However, it seemed to lack some of the same luster that it once possessed when we had originally met. My work days were not boring, and the patients were as kind and generous as always, however there was a certain spark that was missing. I hoped it would pass as quickly as it appeared, that no one else would notice, and that I could move on with my life.

There was also the matter of Randy. Although our relationship was very young, and we were just beginning to try and figure out where we fit into each other's lives, I was unable to envision a world where there was space for all of my men—Logan, Lucas, and Randy. I had been successful in keeping the two youngest attached to a different chapter in my life, but unless I could overlap the two stories, something was going to have to give. I knew what that had to be.

Randy and I had agreed to meet on Friday afternoon for coffee. We were meeting at the same Good Earth where Connie Lewiston and I had met several months earlier to try and work through the difficulties she was having with her husband. I had heard from Connie a few times since she had moved on, and she seemed to be doing well, exhausted but well.

I arrived early in anticipation of our meeting to allow myself time to rehearse the script I had gone over so many times in my head. I knew that this conversation had to be guided by logic, by my mind and not my heart. If I allowed my heart into this, it would not end well. In fact, it was unlikely to end at all if that happened.

I arrived half an hour in advance of our scheduled 10:30 a.m. meeting time. This turned out to be a good decision as Randy walked in through the front door of the café at 10:15 a.m. As soon as our eyes met, I knew this was not going to be easy. I wished I had written everything down that I was planning to say. I would just pull the note out of my pocket, read it out loud, leave the café, and carry on with the rest of my life. I envisioned it might read something like this:

> *Randy,*
> *I am very thankful that you came into my life. These past few months have been wonderful for me. I think you are a very caring and genuine human being, and I have appreciated getting to know the man that you are. Given my present situation, what with my work and trying to raise two young children on my own, I am sure you can appreciate that I have little time for anything else in my life right now. I want you to know that if this were a different time, a different place, things would be different. Now, however, is neither that time nor that place. I thank you for understanding.*

He would surely agree with me, and that would be that. We would shake hands, wish each other well, and walk out of the restaurant laughing about small things like the weather or the current state of the world.

As I looked up at him again, I knew it was not going to be that easy or that scripted.

"Hello, Tori. How have you been the past week?"

"Great! As well as can be expected. Everything seems to be falling nicely into place with the boys. Audrey is also doing well. How about you?"

"I am doing really well. Can I get you something, perhaps a chai tea latte?"

"That would be great."

I watched him make his way over to the counter and

place our order. Something about him seemed different, somewhat sadder than I was used to. His back seemed a little more slouched, and his gait a little less sure of itself. As he turned back towards the table, I could see this also reflected in his eyes.

As he sat down and placed our drinks on the table, a chai tea latte for me and a black coffee with one sugar for himself, he looked at me and said, "We can't do this."

"Can't do what?"

"Whatever this is." He motioned back and forth between us with his right hand.

"What do you mean 'whatever this is?'"

"You know what I mean, Tori. Let's not beat around the bush. I can't continue to be just a part of some of your life. I don't want to be someone who is just fit in here and there. I want to be a real part of your life, your whole life."

Stick to the script, I said to myself, stick to the script. "I am not sure what else I can do right now. I have my work and I have my kids and …"

"Include me in those things! I would hope that you would know by now that I am genuine and that I am holding nothing back. I want to be with you, whatever that looks like. I know it is easier to open the door into my life. My life is much less complex. I get that. I think though that if you tried, really tried, you could see that there could be a place for me. Hell, I might even make your life better, maybe even easier!"

I had a multitude of emotions swirling inside my entire being at that moment—joy, sadness, lust, anger, fear … I decided to go with anger as that was the one that was likely to get me closer to where I needed to go.

"How dare you presume to know what my life is about and think that you could make it easier? My life is extremely complex, and I already have two parts that require my full attention. To think that I would have time for something else is ludicrous."

He didn't flinch. He stood his ground and just looked up at me with an increasing sadness in his eyes. "That is exactly what I knew you were going to say. I am not surprised. I knew that if I didn't give it a shot, I was always going to regret not saying something. I don't want you to think, not for a moment, that I regret a single moment of the time we have spent together. I have loved every minute of it. Even this conversation we are having right now. It reminds me of the type of person you are. The type of person I am falling in love with. I don't want this to be any more difficult for you than it already is. That is why, unless you tell me to stay, for any reason at all, I am going to get up and walk out before either one of us says or does something that will permanently damage what we have had together over this very short time."

He looked over at me, and I said nothing. It was not that I didn't have anything to say. It was all in the fact that my anger had melted away and was being replaced by joy, lust, relief, excitement ... If I said anything, I knew that those emotions would come rising to the surface to invite him back in—invite him back into my entire life, forever. So, I sat there begging my good friend Silence to help me through this as he had done so many times before. I fought back the tears and looked away. I didn't know how long I would be able to fight.

I needn't have worried. As I looked up, I caught the last

of his blond hair and his blue uniform as he rounded the corner out the front door and out of my life. He didn't look back, and he never broke his stride.

I wasn't entirely sure what I had accomplished by sticking with the script. I was sure that this was going to haunt me for a long time, likely for the rest of my life. I got up from the table, moved swiftly through the crowd and entered the women's washroom. I quickly locked myself in the first available stall, and not caring who was around me and within hearing distance, began to heave. I didn't stop until I was sure that my stomach was completely empty. Things were never going to be the same. I flushed the toilet, opened the door to the stall, washed my hands and fought off the tears now streaming down my face. I looked in the mirror and thought, *Dr. Victoria Jones, single mother and surgeon.* I didn't think I recognized the person reflected back at me anymore. It really scared me.

40
Yearning

Life was falling back into a pleasant yet demanding routine after the Christmas holidays. Logan, Lucas and Audrey were starting the New Year off in stride, and I was starting a conversation with my one-, three- and five-year goals after a rocky and ill-defined hiatus. All was as it should be—a balance between my personal life and my professional life. And yet, there was a yearning for something more; something that would make my life so much easier, yet so much more complex and chaotic.

My mind kept wandering back to the night Randy and I had spent together. I was questioning everything about that night and what it had meant in the grand scheme of who I was and especially who I wanted to be. There was little doubt that it had left a strong impression on me, however I was confused as to what direction I should take it from there. Everything I knew about Randy led me to believe that he was a very sincere and caring individual, yet I was still unsure as to where that might fit into the story of our lives. Some days, I wished that I could go back and erase it all, and other days I thought it was one of the most enlightening moments in the past several years of my life.

I had replayed everything about the short lived, ill-fated relationship over and over in my mind a million times. There were multiple acts of fate that had been necessary to bring us together in the first place, including the loss of his pregnant wife in the line of duty, my previous brush with the law and Martin's overwhelming urge for large quantities of narcotics. Was all of this to be for naught? What was the positive that could possibly be found in any of this if not for the continued fanning of a passion that had been successfully ignited between Randy and myself?

But, there was so much to lose. It would be impossible to keep any relationship I might have with Randy separate from my work and my children. How can you build a life with someone where there is so little room and so little time to offer them? What if something happened and the relationship had to end, not only between Randy and myself, but also between Randy and my children? Where would that leave everybody?

Then I would remember how complete and how good I felt whenever I was with Randy, or even when I was just thinking about him. There was a feeling of comfort and contentment I had not felt for a long time, if ever. Most of the pushing had been me against him for more and more space, and he had not argued. He had left as he had promised and had not looked back. He had in fact given me everything I told him I needed. Or so I thought ...

I yearned to be with him. I thought about what I wouldn't give to be sitting by the pond behind the hospital as we had done on that first day when I had found myself starting to be drawn closer to him, or how he had seemed right at home during his first and only visit to my house when we had plied him with cookies and milk and questions, or how he made me feel during the half night we had spent together at his place. No one had ever made love to me as slowly or as precisely as he had that evening. I could not get that out of my mind...

I yearned for him day and night. I found my mind wandering to the night we spent together when I was with patients in clinic, when I was in the operating room and when I was at home with my children. I thought about him when I was alone and when I was with other people—I thought about him day and night. When was this ever going to get any easier? It seemed to consume my very being.

I knew that I was not going to be able to just call him up to find out how he was doing. That was not a simple luxury afforded to those who had insisted on ending an otherwise fabulous relationship. I also knew that any contact I had with him was likely to draw me back in rather than allowing me to gain more distance. What I really wanted was to be able to stop ruminating on him, on us, for at least an hour in any given day. That would be a good start. Once again, my best friend Rosalee was having none of this. She still remained adamant that she would not protect me from him. She was even urging me to continue to see him and explore whether or not we were a good fit.

We were a good fit, dammit, that was the problem!

I could still feel his hands on me, feel his mouth on me and feel the urgency in his voice and his movements from that night not so long ago. It seemed as if it would never leave. I knew in my heart that the complete story had not

Yearning

yet been written. Now I just had to convince my mind of what the possibilities were ...

41

Mommy, Are There More People Like Me?

The next few months were extremely busy, and I was able to keep my mind on the task at hand—improving as a surgeon and improving as a mother—as long as I kept reminding myself that there was no room in our lives for anything or anyone else. Easter had passed without incident, and spring was suddenly upon us. We had settled again into a routine that seemed to fit comfortably for everyone, except me. I wondered if this was what it was like for all single parents—a constant whirlwind of things to do, places to go, people to see, without much time for oneself. Was it just me and the type of person I was, the type of person I had become out of necessity, or was this what it was like for all single parents, especially mothers?

I was still living day to day for the most part. I referred to my goal lists from time to time, when possible. I tried to choose one small thing to move me closer each day.

It was amongst all this routine and chaos that I found myself sitting across from Logan at the breakfast table one morning. It was a lovely spring morning and the sun was streaming in through the large kitchen window. Lucas was not yet awake, and I was taking a few minutes to enjoy an engaging conversation with Logan. He was excited about a field trip to the Calgary Zoo and wondered what animal he most resembled. It was a very animated conversation on his part.

"Mommy, I am a giraffe. I am a tall, thin glass of water!"

We both laughed heartily as this was a phrase I had used often when describing Logan to himself and others. I would say, 'This is my oldest son Logan—he is a tall, thin glass of water!' I could tell that he was pleased with this description of himself. He looked down at his breakfast and started pushing the few Mini-Wheats that remained in his bowl around in their swimming pool of milk.

"Mommy?"

"Yes, Logan."

"Who am I?"

"What do you mean who are you? Why you are Logan, of course! My smart, silly, brave little Logan!"

"No! Who am I? Why do most of my friends have mommies AND daddies, even if they don't live together?"

Ah, I thought, *and so it begins.* I had been waiting for this question for years, and here it was right in front of me. I had read articles, purchased books and spoken endlessly with others who would someday be faced with the same inquiry. I knew only that I was not prepared to lie. While this seemed obvious to some who knew me, others had suggested various types of stories that I might tell or tales that I might weave. Some had suggested, for example, that I reply with 'Your father was killed in a car accident' or 'Your father had to leave for very important work', or my favorite, 'Your father is out there somewhere, Mommy just doesn't know where'. I had even had male friends and acquaintances offer to step up to the plate and be named 'the father' when this question came up. Of course, I had not ever considered any or all of this to be more than just misplaced sentiments on the part of well-intentioned individuals. I knew that the truth was the only way I could maintain my sanity amidst all the chaos. I also knew that I owed it to my children to provide them with the facts and let them determine how the rest of the story would unfold. After all, it was not my life we were speaking about, it was their past, present and future. I firmly believed that their lives were theirs to create. I had taken years to fully prepare myself for this moment, and sitting looking over at my oldest son, I knew that I was going to be winging it for the most part.

"Well..." I began slowly, "You know that Mommy loves you, and your brother, very much. Mommy wanted you very badly, and there was no daddy around. Mommy knew that if she wanted to have you, she would need to have you before she was too old. Do you understand so far?"

"Yes, you wanted me very much!"

"Yes, honey! I loved you before you even arrived, before you were even in my tummy. Mommy found a very nice doctor, and he helped mommy to get you. I got you, but no daddy. I love you very much!"

"Will I ever get a daddy?"

I didn't know how to answer this question. I had no experience with this particular question and how I should answer it. I was not about to promise something that I would never be able to deliver on, however I did not want to leave him without hope.

Mommy, Are There More People Like Me?

"Logan honey, Mommy doesn't know the answer to your question. We will have to wait and see. We never know what is going to happen to us. Mommy will always be here for you. That is all I can promise you. Is that enough for now?"

"Yes. We will have to wait and see!" He reached over and hugged me.

Out of everything that I had ever read on this subject, the only thing that had helped me today was to keep it simple. Logan had not been asking complicated questions about how babies were made when he asked about not having a father; rather he had been asking about the lack of a male role model or father figure in his life. This was a simpler question, but also a more complex one, as it did not have any definitive answers.

Logan got up from the table and ran off to get ready for the day. He seemed happy and content with our short discussion, at least for now. I knew this was likely to be a topic that came up from time to time, from one or even both of my children. It was likely I would have to muddle my way through the answers every time. All I knew for sure was that I was basing my discussions on several principles—that I loved my children very much, that I would always be there for them and that I was never going to lie. I was happy that I had fulfilled all of these goals today.

I took a few minutes to reflect on what might lie ahead for Logan, Lucas and myself. I knew that there were at least forty other children, half siblings, somewhere out there, who shared the same donor as my children. I had already interacted with some of the parents on Facebook and other such web-based sites, although I had not met any of them in person. I knew that the question of 'Who am I, Mommy' would become intimately entwined with this fact as my children got older. As I sat there in the late morning sunlight, I thought that I should write a book about this. I envisioned that it would be a work of fiction that would follow the escapades of a group of donor-related children as they wove their way through the various complex relationships that they would form, amongst themselves and with the outside world. I imagined what I might name such a work of fiction. My mind was wandering to all sorts of possibilities when Logan came around the corner and ran up to plant a big kiss on my cheek. He turned to me and asked, "Mommy, are there more people like me?"

"Yes, Logan, honey," I replied as I hoisted him up on my lap and leaned back into the sunlight.

And there you have it—the perfect name for my first work of fiction: *Mommy, Are There More People Like Me?* It would be my first Dr. Victoria Jones, Single Mother by Choice novel. I promised myself that I would start to work on that any day now, making a mental note to speak with my one-, three- and five-year goals—that is when I finally got around to it!

Printed in Canada